"Hold on, Harry. I can take care of myself."

"Now that I think about it," Harry said, suddenly suspicious, "what are you doing here all alone? Where are your bodyguards? Shouldn't there be a limousine waiting for you, princess? Come to think of it, Allie, where is your husband?"

Althea winced at his use of her nickname, but Harry only laughed. "Sorry. Old habits die hard. All right, Madame Boylan, where is that ambassador husband of yours?"

"Daniel's in Paris, if you must know," she said over her shoulder as she hurried down the airport terminal, not wanting to admit the truth to Harry yet.

When they stood toe-to-toe, Althea could feel Harry's soft breath on her hair. She marveled that the touch of his hand could still make her shiver, that he could so easily elicit a sensual response from her, that ten years apart made little difference.... "Leave me be, Harry. If the snow ruins my shoes, I can always buy another pair."

"Ah, yes, now that's my old Althea. Buy, buy, buy. Everything to be had for a price."

"Not everything," Althea growled. Not by a long shot, she thought...and soon enough Harry would learn just what she was talking about....

Dear Reader,

Get ready to counter the unpredictable weather outside with a lot of reading *inside*. And at Silhouette Special Edition we're happy to start you off with *Prescription: Love* by Pamela Toth, the next in our MONTANA MAVERICKS: GOLD RUSH GROOMS continuity. When a visiting medical resident—a gorgeous California girl—winds up assigned to Thunder Canyon General Hospital, she thinks of it as a temporary detour—until she meets the town's most eligible doctor! He soon has her thinking about settling down—permanently....

Crystal Green's *A Tycoon in Texas*, the next in THE FORTUNES OF TEXAS: REUNION continuity, features a workaholic businesswoman whose concentration is suddenly shaken by her devastatingly handsome new boss. Reader favorite Marie Ferrarella begins a new miniseries, THE CAMEO— about a necklace with special romantic powers—with *Because a Husband Is Forever*, in which a talk show hostess is coerced into taking on a bodyguard. Only, she had no idea he'd take his job title literally! In *Their Baby Miracle* by Lilian Darcy, a couple who'd called it quits months ago is brought back together by the premature birth of their child. Patricia Kay's *You've Got Game*, next in her miniseries THE HATHAWAYS OF MORGAN CREEK, gives us a couple who are constantly at each other's throats in real life—but their online relationship is another story altogether. And in *Picking Up the Pieces* by Barbara Gale, a world-famous journalist and a former top model risk scandal by following their hearts instead of their heads....

Enjoy them all, and please come back next month for six sensational romances, all from Silhouette Special Edition!

All the best,

Gail Chasan
Senior Editor

Please address questions and book requests to:
Silhouette Reader Service
U.S.: 3010 Walden Ave., P.O. Box 1325, Buffalo, NY 14269
Canadian: P.O. Box 609, Fort Erie, Ont. L2A 5X3

PICKING UP
THE PIECES

BARBARA GALE

SPECIAL EDITION

Published by Silhouette Books

America's Publisher of Contemporary Romance

To Gabrielle,
who travels with me to places unknown,
weaving a magical spell of words

Acknowledgments
To Jessica Faust, the best of agents; it's that simple.

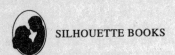 SILHOUETTE BOOKS

ISBN 0-373-24674-9

PICKING UP THE PIECES

Copyright © 2005 by Barbara Gale

This edition published by arrangement with Harlequin Books S.A.

® and TM are trademarks of Harlequin Books S.A., used under license. Trademarks indicated with ® are registered in the United States Patent and Trademark Office, the Canadian Trade Marks Office and in other countries.

Visit Silhouette Books at www.eHarlequin.com

Printed in U.S.A.

Books by Barbara Gale

Silhouette Special Edition

The Ambassador's Vow #1500
Down from the Mountain #1595
Picking Up the Pieces #1674

BARBARA GALE

is a native New Yorker. Married for over thirty years, she, her husband and their three children divide their time between Brooklyn and Hobart, New York. Ms. Gale has always been fascinated by the implications of outside factors, including race, on relationships. She knows that love is as powerful as romance readers believe it is.

She loves to hear from readers. Write to her at P.O. Box 150792, Brooklyn, New York 11215-0792 or visit her Web site at www.barbaragale.com.

Dear Reader

Picking Up the Pieces is the story of love lost, lost opportunities and second chances. It explores not only interracial romance and unwed motherhood, but the price one pays for personal happiness.

We all have hard choices to make as we grow; it is part of the life process. Ideally, they are our own decisions, but sometimes circumstance dictates otherwise. More often than not, it is a combination of the two. Every once in a while, though, we are allowed an opportunity to revisit the past and make some changes. Althea Almott once sacrificed her heart to the well-being of her family. Ten years later, she has a chance of stealing some happiness for herself, if she only has the courage.

Perhaps Althea's story will provide some small comfort as you travel the road to your own destiny.

Much good fortune.

Barbara Gale

Prologue

If he could have one wish, it would be that he were anywhere else. But he wasn't. And neither was she. As Harry watched Althea, wrapped in lush sable, push past the revolving doors of Kennedy Airport, memories rushed to the surface. Carefully he set them aside. She was married now to an ambassador. Still he was left with a breathless feeling. Or was it simply the churning motion of a certain pain that filled his gut whenever he saw her picture in a newspaper or heard a story about her on the radio? Or thought about her? It didn't matter. He knew, he just knew he should run in the opposite direction, but there was no way to stop his foolish feet; they were going to follow her through those shiny brass doors no matter what his common sense told him. Old wounds and his curiosity were a deadly combination.

The huge arrivals terminal was unusually empty. Not many people traveled in January at this time of night. The postholiday letdown, he supposed. The terminal, bigger than a football field, maybe even three or four fields, seemed quieter than he'd ever heard it. A few passengers wandered around aimlessly, a handful of limo drivers held up cardboard signs to attract riders, and a listless cleaning crew droned on. There were more security personnel than anything else. And nobody was going anywhere, because New York City had just been hit with a major snowstorm.

So it was no trouble to trail her out to the concourse. She was standing by a taxi stand, a lone figure fighting the bitter night air, watching the snow fall, no doubt weighing its implication. The way she was searching for a cab, she couldn't know the storm's extent. Judging by her attire, it was likely that she hadn't even known about the weather when she'd taken off. She probably didn't know how lucky she was to have even landed. Just moments ago he'd heard that all incoming flights had been diverted to Boston. But perhaps the most amazing thing was to find himself running into her here in the middle of New York, when there had been so many other more likely venues over the years.

Shifting his duffel bag, he ran a hand through his unruly blond hair and adjusted his well-worn baseball hat. He would try for cool and hope she didn't hear the tremor in his voice. He was thirty-five, after all, and didn't need to sound like a schoolboy, even if he felt like one.

"Well, well, well, what have we here? Althea Almott in the flesh." He watched her spin round, startled. Her look of chagrin made him smile.

"Ah, sweet Althea, is that sigh for me or in spite of me?" he asked, stifling his disappointment. He watched her turn away, her pointy chin high as she tugged her fur coat snugly round her elegant shoulders.

Althea's brown skin might hide her blushes, but he couldn't know how wildly her heart was beating, how she strove to conceal her shock at meeting him. "Do I know you? You don't look familiar. You must be mistaking me for someone else."

"It might be ten years, but I'd know you anywhere, sweetheart. You haven't changed a bit. Not your face, nor your sweet disposition." He grinned.

"Nor yours, Harry," Althea returned, hiding behind a veil of contempt, her sharp eyes sharp taking in his shabby denim jacket and unkempt appearance. Looking tired and in desperate need of a haircut, still, he was as tall as she remembered, as blond and handsome—and just as annoying, judging by the taunt in his voice.

"You don't approve of my sartorial splendor?" Harry mocked, following the drift of her eyes. If only she knew how ill he had been, how exhausted he was at that very moment, wondering how long his legs would last, perhaps she would be more forgiving. But then, they always had fought over the silliest things, and now, after ten years, here they were together two minutes and at each other's throats again. Oh, well. Giving himself a mental shrug, Harry tried for philosophical. "You look great, Althea. Traveling alone?"

Althea shrugged. "And you?"

"As always," he said with a lopsided smile.

"Always? You mean you never married?"

"Nope. Married to my career, maybe. So," he said, switching gears abruptly, "are you looking for a cab? In case you haven't guessed, every available snowplow is busy clearing the runways. They won't get to the streets for hours. I guess that makes me the man of the hour."

"I can wait," she said softly, watching the snow fall hard and furious. Althea knew Harry was speaking the truth, and with every snowflake, she felt her plans slip away. Now that she thought about it, the dark night was as menacing as the snow, and she supposed she was lucky to have landed on the tarmac in one piece.

"What a good idea," Harry drawled. "I'll join you. We can wait out the storm together." He picked up her bag.

"Hold on, Harry. I can take care of that myself." Spend four hours with the only man to ever leave an imprint on her heart? She didn't think so! But the challenge in Harry's overly bright eyes gave Althea pause. Turning back to the road, all she could see was the swirl of snow intent on burying the city. Where once she might have appreciated its pristine elegance, now she was simply annoyed. She couldn't even make out the sidewalk. Ridiculous.

"Now that I think about it," Harry asked, ignoring her comment, "what are you doing out here all alone? Where are your bodyguards? Shouldn't there be a limousine waiting for you, princess? Come to think of it, Allie, where is your husband?"

She winced at his use of her nickname, but Harry only laughed. "Sorry. Old habits die hard. All right, Madame Boylan, where is that ambassador husband of yours?" he repeated, all trace of humor gone.

"Let's have it, Allie. What are you doing stateside? I seem to have missed something, here. Why, pray tell, are you here on the wrong side of the Atlantic, Allie? An ambassador's wife doesn't just wake up one morning and grab a flight to New York, not even for the winter sales at Saks."

"Daniel is in Paris, if you must know," she said over her shoulder as she hurried back into the terminal, her long stride an elegant testimony to her modeling days. And that is all you must know, she vowed silently.

Harry frowned as he chased after her. "Damn it all, Althea, you know you shouldn't run around unescorted. Does the ambassador know you're here by yourself?"

One look at her face told him everything. He clasped his hand on her elbow and effectively trapped her. "Unless I'm mistaken," he said, giving her legs a long glance, "those are custom-made shoes on your lovely feet. Given the weather, you don't seem to have prepared very well for your trip. What's going on, Allie?"

Standing toe-to-toe, Althea could feel Harry's soft breath on her hair. She marveled that the touch of his hand could still make her shiver, that he could so quickly elicit a response from her, that ten years could make little difference. She tried to pull away but Harry's grip was as firm as the glare in his eyes.

"Leave me alone, Harry. I know what I have on my feet," she said crossly. "If I'd had time to listen to the weather report, I would be wearing boots. But I didn't."

No boots, no taxi, just Harry Bensen. Poetic justice, after her mad dash from Paris. Shrugging free of his hand, Althea stepped back and stared up at him proudly. "This is Kennedy Airport. A taxi will turn up eventually, so don't waste your time on my behalf. I can take care of myself."

"Nobody knows that better than I do," Harry agreed crisply. "But those pretty shoes, it would be a pity to ruin them, don't you think?"

"I can always buy another pair."

"Ah, yes, now that's my old Althea. Buy, buy, buy. Everything to be had for a price."

"Not everything," Althea snapped. "Oh, of all the airports in the world… Honestly, Harry, I wish I hadn't met you."

"Your good luck," he snapped, "if only you knew."

"Harry, why don't you simply turn around and walk the other way?"

"And forget I ever saw you?" Harry snapped with an amused smile.

"Something like that." Althea's eyes were hopeful as she forced a plaintive smile to her lips.

"I thought so. Well, it's too late, darling. Your ambassador husband would be furious—and rightly so—if I left you alone like this."

"It doesn't matter what my husband thinks," Althea retorted. "I prefer to wait alone."

"Wait for what?" Harry asked as he held open the terminal door. "Come on, let's go get some coffee. I'm freezing."

Althea's anger was evident as she rushed past Harry, rudely brushing him aside. But Harry was unimpressed. Feeling the onset of a headache, a sure sign that his fever was rising, he wasn't in the mood to argue. "Playing this one close to the breast, Allie?" Watching her flinch, he guessed that his remark hit home. "Ah, the rich and famous at play."

"This is not a game. I do not play games."

"Then times have changed," he retorted, suddenly too tired to take her on. Too bad she didn't understand the facts, or she would appreciate his foul mood. Four months photographing a South American rainforest would exhaust anyone, but one hour with Althea Almott would be just as exhausting. Maybe he should take her advice and move on, pretend he never saw her. The mysterious infection he was fighting that was turning his insides out would be a handicap in dealing with her. And the damned snow was rotten luck when he was weak as could be with no energy to fight the elements. He should have flown to Cancun the way the doctors suggested and slept on the beach until summer.

And the good news was that no reporter was around to take notes. He could just imagine the headlines: Ambassador's Wife Snowbound with Lover.

Harry didn't know whether to laugh or cry. Just look how she sat, perched on the edge of the plastic chair, trying to hide behind those huge rhinestone sunglasses—at three o'clock in the morning, for Pete's sake. As if any reporter worth his salt wasn't going to spot the world's most famous black model—or anybody, for that matter—wrapped in a fifty-thousand-dollar fur coat.

Ex-model, he corrected himself.

Wife, now, to the American ambassador to France. No longer the hillbilly country girl from

Alabama he'd been so wild about a decade ago. Refashioned: buffed and polished till her smooth black skin glowed like a pearl; her long, slender neck dripped with diamonds; her clothes custom-fitted by Versace. Beyond his touch. She was royalty now; she dined with princes.

It was the sight of her fellow passengers scattered around the drafty building, trying to get comfortable in a place designed to keep them moving, that finally convinced Althea she really was stuck at the airport. Her frustration was clear. She removed her sunglasses to reward Harry with a long, hard stare. "Harry, your concern is commendable, but I didn't ask for your help, and I surely don't appreciate your lousy mood. Like I said before, why don't you put down my bag and disappear?"

Her thick-lashed amber eyes may have made her famous, but flashing as they were, Harry was immune. "Althea, honey, I swear I would if I could, but my conscience would never let me sleep. There's about two, maybe three more inches of snow due to come down before this storm is done, so like it or not, we're stuck with each other. So, what's it going to be? How would you like to play this out?" Harry gave her a long searching look.

He watched as she considered the question, her beautiful face a portrait of uncertainty as she scanned the terminal, looking for an alternative. In the end, he merely shrugged. "All right, Allie, a compromise.

We hang out together, and I ask no questions. That way my conscience won't bother me, and your privacy won't be invaded."

Flopping down beside her, he suddenly didn't want any answers. He was too busy trying to deny the band of sweat that had broken out across his brow, trying to force down the bile rising in his throat, control the furious way his head was spinning. Christ, was he really going to embarrass himself right there in the terminal? Hell, there was no way he was going to make it home if this kept up. Why weren't the damned pills working?

Althea...

But he couldn't work words past his parched lips.

Althea...my head...I can't breathe... Althea, stop swaying...

Althea...

Chapter One

The waiting room in Elmhurst Hospital was chilly and poorly lit, but Althea didn't mind. She had her fur coat to warm her and hospital protocol to distract her. Waiting for an ambulance at the snowbound airport had been a major distraction of worry, too, but eventually it arrived to whisk them away. Then the paperwork, and all those questions for which she didn't have answers. But as long as they were tending to Harry Bensen, wherever he was, having been swallowed up by the medical machine, she didn't care what the admitting nurse wrote down.

How strange it had been to run into him. *Of all people,* didn't one always say? Old lover, lost love.

The set of his shoulders, the way he walked, the tilt of his head, the color of his hair. Had he honestly thought she could ever forget? A woman never forgot her first love. Never.

When finally she was allowed to see him, every inch of Harry's torso was wired to various monitors, and an IV was dripping magical curatives into his arm. Although Althea was able to smile with some measure of relief, she couldn't help noticing how frail he seemed, lying against the starched linen of the hospital bed, his lips white and chapped, the rest of him an alarming shade of yellow. Fighting an odd impulse to brush her lips across his brow, she instead allowed her fingers to skim his burning temple. Harry's eyes fluttered at the featherlight touch.

"Hey soldier, how are you feeling?" she whispered.

Depleted by his illness, tremendously dehydrated, and dazed by the drugs dripping into his arm, Harry was grateful to feel a cool hand on his body. Barely able to open his eyes, his smile was tenuous as he fought the surge of happiness he felt when he saw who was standing by his bedside.

Althea leaned over him, her concern plain as she brushed his hair from his forehead. Obviously fighting, too, an ineffable sadness. "Oh, Harry, why didn't you tell me how sick you were? No, don't answer that," she hushed him with a timid smile. "It was my fault, I had no idea, I should have noticed. Malaria.

Who would have thought? You sure scared the heck out of me, back at the airport, collapsing like that without any warning."

"Next time…I'll send…a telegram."

"I wish you would," Althea admonished him tenderly, recalling her horror as Harry had slid to the cold ground, a ballet in slow motion. "Never mind. The doctors aren't quite sure what you have but they're pumping you up with antibiotics. Your blood count is high so they're running a few tests, but they do promise you a full recovery. They said you have to take better care of yourself, though. No more trips to steamy climates, for one thing."

"They…said so?"

"That and more, way more than I should know about your body," she teased gently. "I think they assume I'm your wife."

"You didn't correct them?"

"The path of least resistance." She thought he was smiling but couldn't be sure, his lips were so cracked. It probably hurt to speak, it probably hurt for him to move anything, given his high fever.

"Hush now, I'll do all the talking." Gently she pressed a piece of ice to his parched mouth. With the lightest touch she bathed his face and hands with a wet washcloth, trying to cool him down. Eventually he seemed to be more comfortable. You poor guy, she thought, what on earth have you been doing to get to this point? I sure hope this is the worst you're going to go through. But she knew that was wishful thinking; she hadn't seen anyone this ill in ages.

Not wishing to disturb him, but unwilling to leave him alone, Althea sat by his side for an hour, until a nurse came to check on his IV. Although the nurse told her she could stay as long as she liked, Althea knew she still had to battle the snow and figured this was a good time to leave. Quietly she gathered her belongings.

"I think I'll be getting home, now that he's safely settled," she whispered.

His head barely turning, Harry's eyes flickered open when he heard the scrape of her chair.

"You'll come back?" he begged hoarsely as he followed her with his eyes.

How could she refuse? Nodding, Althea pressed his hand gently, ignoring the wrench in her heart.

Once, long ago, when she'd had choices to make, Harry Bensen had been one of them. Leaving him behind had not been the high point of her life, and she would never fool herself that he forgave her. Looking down now at his ravaged body covered with wires, she knew all he wanted was a lifeline to the outside world. Glancing at the machines surrounding his bed, monitors attuned to his every heartbeat, an oxygen tank helping him to breathe, she could appreciate that. All right, then, she would give him what she could, and maybe—in the smallest way, of course—it would make up for what she had refused him in the past. Giving in to her impulse, she lowered her lips to kiss his brow and promised to return.

Dawn was breaking as Althea left the hospital. A path plowed by the maintenance crew enabled her to make her way to the express bus, the only vehicle big and heavy enough to dare the city streets after such a storm. Glittering with six inches of newly fallen snow, New York was a prism of beauty now that the sky had cleared, and as the bus lumbered into Manhattan, she was treated to the sight of a skyline that seemed just short of unearthly. Against the expanse of white snow that covered the buildings and floated on the river, a red-orange sun was creeping into the early-morning sky, painting the city with a Technicolor wand. For one brief moment, suspended as she was between her old life and new, Althea wondered if the sight was an omen. It pleased her to think it was.

The bus left her two blocks from her West Side co-op, but treading carefully, she managed to make her way home. It had been nearly a year since she had been back, but Broadway seemed the same. She dashed through the heavy brass doors of the lobby, hungry for its familiar warmth.

In the year she had been gone, its ornate vestibule remained unchanged. Heavy gold-framed mirrors still decorated the walls; the vestibule was still crowded with cabbage-rose sofas and fake greenery. Its familiarity was a comfort, and yet a strong sense of disquiet disturbed her as the doorman greeted her uncertainly. He was new and didn't know who she was. He saw only a black woman rushing through the door, tracking snow into his immaculate lobby. Scrambling to his feet, he gave her a hesitant smile, but she noticed that, very tactfully, he blocked her path.

She watched as he assessed her. A black woman. That was mainly what he saw.

"Ma'am?"

Althea sent him a cool nod, his single word a question she refused to answer. Exhausted, her feet like icicles, and half sick with worry about Harry, she was not in a tolerant mood. Her eyes glacial slits, she could almost read his mind, as he tried to figure her out. Could she live there? She could be a visitor. Maybe a maid using the wrong entrance? No, not a maid, not wearing that fur coat. No, she was definitely not someone's maid. She was too young and pretty, no, definitely not a maid. He stepped aside and let her pass. You never knew.

"I live here," she said tersely as the elevator door closed on his red face.

Shaking with anger, Althea rode the elevator to her floor. The way the doorman had stopped her, stared at and assessed her had been humiliating. Having developed the technique of the cold stare to enormous success, she was not as vulnerable as she used to be, but the assessment was something that, although it happened from time to time, she could never get used to. It happened in stores, in restaurants, in so many countless places. When she stared back, she felt as if she was maintaining her dignity, but it didn't make these confrontations any less painful, or the young man's rudeness any less distressing.

Her distress was twofold. The forbidding silence of the apartment, after she found her keys and let herself in, felt symbolic of her life. She berated herself for being melodramatic, but the feeling would not leave. The silence of the future stretching out before her was a question mark that hovered in the air, not easily dismissed now that she was home. The faint, musty odor of disuse that greeted her, the hollow click of her heels on the cold tile floor were unnerving. She was glad to tug free of her ruined shoes and toss them in a corner, shrug off her coat and turn the thermostat to high.

Nothing had to be decided in a day, a week or even a month, she told herself, as she made her way from room to room, turning on the lights. The workaholic in her was making such unreasonable demands, she knew, as she switched on her bedroom light. Her favorite room, it was done up—unabashedly—in every shade of pink imaginable, lacy and feminine, hers alone. With its pale-pink quilt and featherbed, throw pillows scattered everywhere, a pile of books always at the ready on her night table.

It was her safe haven. The custom-made makeup table with its fully lighted mirror made it her work space at the same time.

Plowing through one of the huge bedroom dressers, Althea searched for a favorite pair of cashmere socks she hoped were still buried beneath the pile of stockings. She might be meticulous with her public appearance, but when she was home alone, with no obligations to fill, makeup never touched her face, and it was sweatpants and socks, all the way.

Taking the opportunity to change and get comfortable, she wandered into her office and plugged in the phone machine. Calling the supermarket down the block, she asked them to send up some milk and butter, a piece of cheddar cheese, a loaf of sourdough bread and a few oranges—until she could get to the supermarket herself. She placed a Post-it note on the refrigerator to call Kennedy Airport in the morning and have them forward her luggage. In the chaos of Harry's fainting spell she had left her luggage behind. A cursory look through the kitchen cupboards revealed a canister of English Breakfast tea. Tried and true, it would go well with a long soak in a hot bath, before she crawled into bed.

Thirty minutes later, surrounded by pale-pink marble and gleaming brass fixtures, the scent of bath oil heavy in the humid air, Althea sank low into the tub. She almost fell asleep, it was so heavenly to lose herself in the bubbles, but the mental notes kept piling up, and she finally gave in to them. No doubt it was a form of regaining control. After her ex-husband's domineering ways, it would be a relief to begin making her own decisions again. She had abrogated so much to him, when they married.

Thus she made a mental note to call her mother, who was probably wondering where she was and not above calling Althea's friends or, worse yet, her ex-husband. Safely tucked away in a pretty house twenty miles outside Birmingham, Alabama, Mrs. Almott still kept close tabs on her only child. The waters Althea traveled were muddy, as her mother was always quick to point out.

In a few days, when she was rested, it might be a good idea to call her old agency, too, and ask her long-time agent, Connie Niles, to start booking her some modeling assignments again. She and Connie had been together forever, since Althea first arrived in New York. Althea had signed with Connie for the simple reason that Connie could be trusted to look out for her interests—Connie was African-American, too. Having just opened her agency, Connie had been on the lookout for new faces. One look at Althea's tall elegant frame, creamy black skin and slanted, golden eyes, and Connie had offered to take Althea all the way to the top with her, if she wanted to come along for the ride. It had taken two years, but things had turned out just as Connie promised. The Niles Model Agency was now one of the most respected agencies worldwide, and that was saying a great deal in an industry that was predicated on whimsy.

So, yes, she would call Connie. And she would call up some of her old friends, drop by some of her old haunts. A long look at her hands and she knew that a manicure was in order, too. She must find a decent gym to join, also. A gym, not a sports club. Her body was her meal ticket; these things must be seen to. She would begin her life anew, and maybe, just maybe, things would work out this time. And if the image of Harry Bensen flashed before her eyes to distract her, she was quick to tamp it down.

Unfortunately, he resurfaced in her dreams, reliving the moment at the airport, when, distracted by her arrival, her belongings, the snow, she looked up to see who called her name. When she discovered Harry standing there, so absolutely disheveled, his unruly blond hair brushing his shoulders, his incandescent-blue eyes shining with the pleasure of their meeting. When her heart had soared at the sight of his familiar, silly half smile. The all-too-brief moment when the years dropped away and they were young again and loved each other so much, the smallest smile a wordless poem.

The next time Althea visited Harry, she found him far more alert. Whatever they were pumping into his veins had begun to kick in. His blue eyes positively glittered as she kissed his cheek lightly.

"I see you've begun to eat," she said, noting the food tray set aside.

"I guess. Just clear soup and Jell-O, though," he grumbled, struggling to sit upright.

Althea wouldn't allow it. "No way, Harry. You stay where you are, and I'll sit here beside you. Let's not have any unnecessary movement. Look, I've brought you tons of magazines and a crossword puzzle book."

Harry's lack of enthusiasm was pronounced.

"For when you're feeling better," she said quickly as she set them aside.

"You know…" He smiled, his eyes an impish twinkle. "When you're close up, like this… That purple sweater looks great on you. And I like your gold braids, but what happened to your long, black curls? I liked them, too."

"Perhaps the lovely lady likes to stay current with the latest styles."

Startled by a deep voice, they turned to find a huge man standing in the doorway. Not particularly handsome, yet with a presence that was unmistakable, his dark skin fortold his African heritage. The wide smile that reached his twinkling brown eyes told of his good nature.

"Hello, Harry."

Harry's mouth curved into a sulk. "Leonel. It's about time you showed. I was going to call your office, again."

"I missed you, too, pal." Smiling faintly, Leonel's long stride made the trip to Harry's bedside in five quick steps. "Here you go. A little something to cheer you up."

Dropping a scrawny bunch of yellow carnations on Harry's bed, Leonel turned the full force of his charming smile on Althea. "You look familiar," he said, extending his hand. "I'm Leonel Murray, Harry's editor at Torregan Publishing."

"And erstwhile friend," Harry muttered, but they both politely ignored him.

"Hi, I'm Althea Almott, an old friend of Harry's. I was at the airport when he collapsed."

"Ah, yes, the model," Leonel said with a snap of his fingers, "and Good Samaritan. A lucky thing for Harry that you were there. A real pleasure, Miss Almott, a real pleasure. And Harry's right, by the way, that shade of lavender becomes you."

"Why, thank you, Mr. Murray."

"Leonel. Please, call me Leonel. And as for you, my invalid friend… 'Erstwhile,' is it?" He laughed. "Is that in the dictionary? It sounds more like an island in the Caribbean."

"Yeah, well, you think the world begins and ends in the Caribbean."

His laugh warm and rich, Leonel explained Harry's remark to Althea's puzzled look. "I was born in Antigua. I miss it, that's what Harry means."

Althea's brow smoothed. "Oh, I've been to Antigua, it's absolutely lovely. I don't blame you for being homesick. The people, the weather, the flowers, the beaches, the food."

"I can see you've been there."

"Many times."

"Me, too. I go back whenever I can. As a matter of fact, my parents still live there. I've asked them many times to come here, but they'll never move. The idea of snow appalls them. They—"

"Excuse me?" Harry piped up feebly. "I hate to interrupt, but is anybody here to visit Harry Bensen, the patient in Room 826?"

"Ah, yes," Leonel said with a wink to Althea as he turned to Harry. "Harry, old man, how *are* you? I got your message, and here I am, ready to spread cheer. How are you feeling?"

"Lousy," Harry said, clearly in a sulk.

"Well, that's good, that's good," said Leonel with a smile. "Why else would you be here? And, yes, I got your message. You have some film for me. Hiding the cannisters under your pillow, laddie?"

"They're in that locker in my duffel bag. My God, what took you so long? They could have been stolen, for all you care."

"Now, who would want to steal a hundred canisters of film?" Leonel asked, the metallic locker door jangling his words. "It's not like they have any value except to you and Torregan Publishing."

"Leonel, did the possibility of their being damaged never occur to you? My cameras are in there, too, and six thousand dollars worth of lenses. They could have been stolen. Take that stuff home with you, will you, for safekeeping?"

"No problem." Carefully, Leonel removed Harry's heavy duffle bag from the hospital locker and began to search through its contents. The camera and satchel of film were easily found. "Tell you what, Harry," Leonel said, as he placed the bags by the bed, "how about I treat you to the film development? As a get-well present."

"Tell you what, Leonel, you're *supposed* to pay for the development. It's in my contract."

Althea watched as the two men traded bantering quips, obviously enjoying themselves. Something told her it was not the first time, either.

"Tell you what," Leonel said as he shouldered the heavy satchel filled with Harry's camera equipment and film when a nurse came to tell them visiting hours were over. "You take your medicine like a good little boy, and I'll have the proofs ready for you in a few days."

"Is that a promise? Seriously? I'm anxious to see what I have."

"Me, too. I have a Pulitzer in mind for you."

Tired as he was, Althea could tell that Harry was pleased by Leonel's announcement. "A Pulitzer prize?" she marveled. "Is Harry that good?"

"Harry's *that* good." Leonel promised, suddenly

serious, "and it's about time the rest of the world knew it. He did some terrific stuff on volcanic activity two years ago at Mauna Loa, and I'm hoping that this next series is every bit as good, if not better. As long as I get the dedication, he can have the prize."

Chapter Two

Althea must have had a hundred errands to run, but, desperate for distraction, she decided to treat herself to a trip to Soho, to check out the designer boutiques. February Fashion Week was approaching, and the store displays would change as a result. A business call, she told herself, to see how up-to-date New York was, in terms of fashion.

She hadn't been to New York in over a year; Paris had spoiled her. Spending the morning skirting slush and piles of dirty snow, she browsed through the stores, fingering the latest silk imports, talking trade with the store owners and admiring their displays. She needn't have worried, New York was still the fashion capital of the world. Wending her way to Prince Street, she was just about to enter the Prada flagship store when she heard a soft voice call her name, the southern drawl familiar to her ears.

"Althea Almott, as I live and breathe. It is you, isn't it?"

Althea disliked autograph hounds, but she was never, ever rude to her fans. Pasting on a practiced smile, she turned around to find herself staring into the past.

Benicia Ericson had been a close childhood friend back in Alabama. Living on the same street, they had gone to the same schools, shopped at the same stores, attended the same birthday parties and shared their most intimate, girlish secrets. The pair had been inseparable. Things had only started changing when they were midway through high school and began fantasizing about their future. Althea dreamed of going to New York and searching out the bright lights. Less adventuresome, Benicia had felt threatened by her best friend's plans to leave and when Althea left, it was on the heels of Benicia's adolescent anger.

Ten years later, standing on Broadway, they eyed each other warily. Looking down at the tiny brown-skinned woman, Althea was hard put to recognize her old friend. A floppy, gray wool hat nearly hid Benicia's entire face, but that familiar high-pitched laugh was a giveaway.

"Benicia Ericson! Of all people to meet in Soho."

"Birmingham does seem a long way away," Benicia agreed, as they shared an awkward embrace.

"Two thousand miles and two hundred years. How *are* you, Benicia?"

"Oh, I'm fine, thanks. But I don't have to ask how you're doing."

"Yes, I'm fine," Althea said quickly. "My goodness, though, what on earth are you doing in New York?"

"I live here."

Althea was surprised. "No! How come I don't know that?"

"Maybe because we don't eat in the same restaurants?" Benicia teased, then turned serious. "And maybe because I never called you. You're such a big star, I just couldn't bring myself to…impose."

A little embarrassed, Althea shook her head. "Well, it's good to see you, Benicia. Do you ever get back home? To Alabama, I mean."

"I haven't been back in years," Benicia admitted. "But I don't know if that's good or bad."

"Me, neither, I'm sorry to say. My mom still lives there, though, a few miles outside the city. And yours?"

"Oh, she's still there, holding down the fort. I left soon after you did and never went back, either. And I never will."

"Something in the water?" Althea grinned.

"Something," Benicia said, smiling back. "Do you ever seriously consider returning?"

"Sure I do. Lately, I think about it a lot."

"Not me, girlfriend. But I've thought about you. Sometimes, thinking about you was the only thing that kept me going. I'd read about you in the paper and think, *Why, I know that girl, and if she can do it...* You know the sort of thing, silly stuff, but it gave me hope. My friend the world-class model, practically a movie star. Oh, my, yes, I gave you *lots* of thought. I still do, every time I see a magazine with your face on the cover, wearing that famous ruby-red lipstick."

"I'm paid to wear that lipstick, you know."

"I figured as much. So, what have you been up to? I haven't seen your picture lately. Oh, wait, I remember. You hooked up with the good-looking brother from Long Island, that Boylan ambassador fellow, if I remember correctly. Married yourself a real live prince, straight out of Cinderella, and went to live in Europe somewhere."

Althea's amber eyes held a faint glint of humor. "Paris, actually."

"Paris," Benicia sighed. "Imagine that, your whole life has been one big fairy tale, hasn't it? Just like you said it would be. It just goes to show, a small-town girl really can make good in this nasty old world."

"Oh, Benicia, fairy tales don't always end happily. My husband and I—our divorce was finalized a few weeks ago. It just hasn't hit the papers yet."

"No!"

"Yes."

"Oh, my, I'm so sorry, Althea."

"It's all right, Benicia." Althea blinked. "How could you know? You would have soon enough, in any case. It will be in all the papers soon."

"Is that why you're here in New York?"

"Actually, I only just got back a few days ago."

"And you run into me and my big mouth. Like I said, I'm really, really sorry."

"Don't be. Things happen."

"Too true," Benicia said thoughtfully. "Say, listen, I was just window shopping, stalling for time. I have a free hour before I have to go to a meeting. Do you have time for a cup of coffee, catch up on old times? Unless—" Benicia hesitated "—you're busy. You're probably busy."

"I'm not too busy for an old friend," Althea said firmly. "And a cup of tea sounds perfect."

The two women made their way a few blocks over to Houston Street, laughing over silly memories that began immediately to surface. Althea talked her friend into having lunch at a small Ethiopian restaurant that served an excellent tea, and tiny glasses of Tej, Ethiopia's popular honey wine. It wasn't long before the years fell away and they grew comfortable with each other, although Benicia was careful to stay away from the subject of her friend's divorce.

"So, tell me," Benicia asked, as the Tej began to warm them, "you were always talking about going to New York to become a model. Was it worth it?"

"Well, it wasn't like I was any sort of scholar back in Birmingham, just another pretty girl with a good body and interesting eyes. But my mom lives in a real nice house now with an honest-to-goodness white picket fence and a garden, which is all she ever wanted. So, yes, it was worth it. Of course, it wasn't without its difficulties. But, hey, that's a conversation for another day. Let's talk about you. You look terrific, you know. The same, but different."

She meant it, too. Benicia looked great. The glossy black curls Althea remembered from their childhood were now worn in a tight cap, her brow was a delicate thin arch over her big, olive-black eyes, and the flirty, long gold earrings she favored set off her graceful neck.

"I do try to take care of myself," Benicia grimaced with good humor.

"So, are you going to tell me how *you* landed in New York, considering how angry you were when I left."

"Considering?" Benicia repeated as their waiter arrived with two steaming bowls of Chicken Wat stew. "Oh, this smells so good."

"I thought you would like it. It's my favorite."

"I can see why," Benicia said as she picked up her spoon. "But do you mean to say that you don't follow the Birmingham gossip?" she asked, returning to her thread of thought. "Your momma never told you?"

"Like I said, my mother doesn't live in the old neighborhood anymore. But now you've got my curiosity up, what don't I know?"

Neatly putting aside her spoon, Benicia rummaged about in the huge tote bag at her feet until she found her wallet. Opening it carefully, she drew out a slender folio of photographs and handed it to Althea. "His name is James. He's nine years old and he is the most important thing in my life. He *is* my life."

"Oh, Benicia, he's adorable. I didn't know you were married."

Benicia's eyes grew slanted. "I never said I was married."

"But—"

"The brother had plans," Benicia said coolly as she quickly retrieved her son's pictures and stuffed them back in her bag. "Unfortunately, they didn't include fatherhood. So, it seems we're both single women, aren't we?"

Althea fiddled with her silverware, unsure what to say.

Observing her friend's discomfort, a flash of amusement flitted across Benicia's round face. "Althea Almott, if I didn't know better, I'd believe you were blushing. The Alabama in a girl never quite disappears, does it?"

Althea was surprised by Benicia's observation. No matter how hard she tried to leave the South behind, Alabama did live just below the sophisticated surface she had worked so hard to acquire—a multi-layered conservatism that kept her slightly off balance.

"Oh, Althea, I'm only teasing you," Benicia said, patting her friend's hand gently. "I don't complain about being a single mom. I've had a long time to figure things out. You don't remember what a stubborn kid I was, always having to learn things the hard way."

Confused, Althea sent her a curious look. "How do you mean?"

"I got pregnant," Benicia said bluntly. "Soon after you left." For one brief moment, her soft voice was wistful. "I had plans, but then real life had a way of intruding."

"Oh, there's truth to that, all right," Althea agreed sadly. "But what happened to James's dad?"

"A really good question, for which I have a really dumb answer. I made it easy for him. I let him go. Nobody had to do *me* any favors! I *knew* how to take care of myself. Mistake number one was letting him *have* his way. Mistake number two was letting him *get* away."

"Do you ever see him?"

Benicia shook her head. "I wanted him to stay, and I think he did, too. Lordy, that man swore up and down the Mississippi that it wasn't *me*. But I was pregnant…. I think he panicked, but how could I blame him? He was only a kid himself, gone before I even started showing. The oldest story in the world, isn't it?" Benicia said with a sad sigh. "Oh, well, all that's history, now. But something told me to have this baby, which I did. All by myself."

"All by yourself?" Althea repeated with a frown. "Your family didn't help? Where was your mother?"

"Come on, Althea, you remember my momma. When she found out I was pregnant, she beat the living daylights out of me, then she kicked me out of the house. Nowadays, things are different, but back then…" She raised her wineglass, an ironic smile on her face. "To small towns."

"And to James," Althea added quickly.

"Thank you." Benicia nodded as they clicked glasses. "To the future president of the United States." She laughed. "This week, anyway. If he runs true to form, he'll want to be a brain surgeon by next week. But, hey, enough of me. What about you, the big star and all?"

"A *small* star in a firmament of thousands."

"Oh, I don't know about that. You are so famous, I can't help but tell everyone I know you. And they always know who I'm talking about."

"Well, that's sweet, but I've been away awhile. I don't know how long you shine in that firmament."

"The public's memory isn't that short. You should know. So, where do you go from here?"

"I have some decisions to make. But right now I have to call it a day," she said, pushing back her chair. "I left about four tons of mail sitting on my dining room table waiting to be sorted, not to mention three hundred phone calls I have to make."

"Getting back into the routine?" Benicia laughed.

"It will take a few weeks," Althea said. "Will I see you again? Will you call me, if you have a chance? We can't not see each other another ten years. And I would like to meet James."

"I'll call," Benicia said vaguely.

Althea got into a cab, wondering if she would. She rode back home, her head filled with thoughts of Alabama, memories she usually preferred not to examine suddenly clamoring for attention…

Her mother leaving every night at nine to work the night shift at a local factory so she could be around Althea during the day; standing in line every other Monday, rain or shine, waiting with her mother for their food stamps; Tuesdays, free cheese distribution at the welfare center; Thursdays, the day stale bread was distributed by a nearby package outlet, and if Althea had been *really* good that week, *if* she had passed all her tests in school, her mother gave her fifty cents to buy a box of stale cupcakes.

All her mother's hard work scrimping, Althea thought bitterly, and the most they had ever had to show for it? An ugly shack with four unpainted walls that barely supported a tin roof. The day Althea handed her mother the keys to a little red brick house, they had stood together on the porch and cried. They didn't need words to know how far they had come, how long the walk had been. Her mother's first steps into her new home had been Althea's proudest moment.

Had it been worth it?

Yes, she thought, thinking back to Benicia's question as she entered her apartment thirty minutes later. Throwing her keys in the blue Depression-glass bowl that sat on a gleaming refectory table, hanging her fur coat in the huge cedar closet, putting the tea to boil on her Viking stove. Yes, she thought, as she looked out at the view over the brawniest city in the world—and she a part of it—yes, it had been worth it.

Chapter Three

Althea left the Niles Model Agency shell-shocked. Numb with disappointment, she stumbled twice in the snow, she was so distraught. Suddenly the sun wasn't so bright, the city's hoary skyscrapers seemed as gray as her prospects. If she hadn't been afraid to rash her cheeks with salty tears, she would have cried.

The only thing that saved her from a complete breakdown was the sight of Harry Bensen when she arrived at Elmhurst Hospital, soon after the disastrous interview with her old employer. When she walked into his hospital room, her arms filled with flowers, he was sitting up, dozing against some pillows.

"Harry?" she whispered. Slowly he opened his eyes. They were still glassy, but he did seem more alert. Hollowed as they were, they could not hide the beautiful curve of his smile or the deep cleft of his chin when he saw who had arrived.

"Althea? I know you said you would stop by," he whispered, "but I just assumed you were being polite."

Carefully Althea set the flowers on the windowsill. "Harry Bensen," she said lightly as she shrugged off her coat. "Weak as can be, mouthy as ever." Coming on top of her disastrous visit to the Niles Model Agency, Althea was hurt by his seeming rejection and resolved to make this a quick visit.

Harry's lips stretched into a lopsided grin, and his voice grew stronger as he spoke. "And you. Still as beautiful as ever. And look, yellow roses, in the middle of winter. Thank you."

"You're welcome."

"I'm grateful to you, coming all the way from Manhattan to see me."

"My pleasure." She had to admit he looked very appealing lying there in the hospital camouflage that did very little to conceal the hard planes of his body. Whatever disease he was harboring had not affected his appeal. Throwing her coat across the back of a chair, Althea gingerly approached the edge of the bed. "You're looking much better, Mr. Bensen."

"I feel better, even if it has been a long couple of days."

"I'll just bet. Tell me, how long were you sick before you collapsed? You must have been ill on the plane. Didn't you realize?"

"Oh, I knew what was happening, but I tried to fight it. I was on a shoot in northwest Brazil when I took sick, about thirty miles outside of Manaus. That's a small town on the Amazon River. Do you have any idea how hard it is to get there?"

"What, no subway?" Althea asked, her eyes wide with mischief.

"It must not have been running," Harry drawled. "Anyhow, there I was, in the middle of nowhere, boiling my water like a good boy, and I'd had all my shots, and I was careful what I ate…. I guess my resistance was low. I started getting headaches…then chills…. The initial attack wasn't too bad, I thought I had malaria at first, but the doctors in Manaus assured me it was just a garden-variety virus. I had a bout with malaria years ago and once you've had malaria, you're susceptible to its reoccurrence. I was prepared for it, too. Malaria, that is. I had my meds in my backpack and plenty of aspirin. Let's just say the quinine wasn't working as fast as it should. Turns out it wasn't working because whatever I have, it's not malaria, thank God."

"But when you knew you were getting worse, don't you think you should have left Brazil?"

"Hey, I was in the middle of some really interesting work. I'm trying to get a handle on the rainforest decimation in that area. It's going to be a real scandal when the word gets out, let me tell you, and with a book coming out—well, it's *supposed* to come out this spring—my photographs are going to be the centerpiece. It was way important to finish the job and I had so little left to do. Like I said, it's not the easiest thing in the world to fly back and forth to South America. We won't even talk about the cost of the plane fare. To be honest, though, I barely made it back to Manaus. From there, I was lucky enough to grab a boat up the Amazon to Macapa. I only left Manaus in the first place because my hands were shaking so much I could hardly hold my camera steady."

"Harry, how unwise."

"Yeah, I know. I spent a week in Macapa General Hospital, but when I got the chance to jump a military transport back to the States, I took it. I had just landed—flown twenty-two hours, nonstop—when I ran into you."

"But you have your pictures," Althea said with a sad shake of her head.

"I have my pictures," Harry agreed, "that's the important thing. You know I hate to say it, Allie, I know I'm the one who's sick, but you're looking a little off yourself. Is anything wrong? You never did tell me why you were back in the States."

So much for spending two hours in front of her mirror, Althea thought. She affected innocence, but Harry wasn't fooled.

"Come on, Allie, I won't give away your secrets. You always had a certain look when you were upset. Watching you frown, I remembered." The worry in her eyes was more than apparent, it lived in a tiny crease above her brow.

"I have no secrets."

Suddenly overcome by an explosive cough, Harry didn't challenge her. Frightened, Althea held a glass to his lips and he managed to take a few sips before collapsing back on his bed. "It's okay… I'm okay. Thanks. They're not sure, they took X-rays, I may have a touch of pneumonia."

"A touch of pneumonia," Althea gasped. "Next time, I'll bring cough drops instead of flowers. Do you want me to call a nurse?"

"No, don't, please, don't. I'm medicated to the gills, and they're so busy, as it is. Tell me about yourself, instead," Harry insisted as he lay back and closed his eyes. "That will distract me."

Althea hesitated, unsure what to do. Harry was white as a ghost from the coughing spell. Smoothing his sheets back into order, she gave in gracefully. Privately, she decided that if he had another coughing fit, she would not ask his permission to ring for a nurse.

"Sometimes," she said with a shake of her head, "I think I should save the paparazzi some legwork and send out bulletins, the way my life is scrutinized by the tabloids."

"I've noticed," Harry said with a small smile, opening his eyes a crack.

"Oh, not you, too?" she wailed in mock horror.

"I can't help it. Your face stares back at me from every magazine rack, across every cash register, in every supermarket in this country. Whenever I buy a quart of milk I get an update on your life."

"You just can't help reading those tabloids, hmm, even knowing that most of what they print isn't true?"

"Not me!" Harry protested, but the smile on his lips belied his promise. "Don't worry, I don't believe half of it. Mostly, I just look at the pictures, I don't buy them."

"No one does."

Harry's sudden bark of laughter was a welcome surprise. "Yeah, well... Of course, it's been a long time since I bought a quart of milk. So, let's see, what's it been, eight, ten years since we've laid eyes on each other? Or is it that I just read about you so much that I feel like I've seen you more often?"

"Who can say? I don't keep track of those kinds of things."

"Is that what I was, a kind of thing?" Harry spoke so casually, Althea missed the probing glint in his eyes.

"An hour or so with an old friend, shall we leave it at that?"

"That would be nice, Allie, Auld Lang Syne and all that, if I didn't know that sentiment was not your strong point."

Althea was taken aback. "Harry, how can you say something like that?" But she knew what he meant. They were not old friends, he was not the guy that got away, he was the one who had been shown the door. She started to rise, but Harry quickly reached for her hand.

"Please, don't go. That was rude of me and I apologize. I swear not to say another nasty word."

Althea hesitated, of two minds whether to stay. "All right, I'll chalk it up to your fever—but only this once," she warned.

"Scout's honor, Allie, I'll be nice. Come on, bring me up-to-date. Why the sad look?"

Althea wasn't sure she wanted to explain, but her down-turned mouth spoke volumes. "Do you remember Connie Niles?"

Unpleasant memories darkened his eyes. "Quite well. She was no fan of mine, and if I remember correctly, the feeling was mutual. Connie had a real attitude about my dating you, which she never bothered to hide. I used to think she disapproved of my skin color—or the lack, therein."

"Connie was looking out for my interests. She never approved of interracial dating. She used to say that white men dated black women for—"

"For?"

Heat stole to her face. "I'm embarrassed to say."

"Say it."

"Um, I think the expression is 'brown sugar'...."

Harry was appalled. "And you believed her?"

"Oh, like that was unheard of?" she retorted impatiently. "In any case, I was young, and everything Connie said was the gospel."

"Everything Connie Niles said was vulgar!"

"Look, Harry, can we not go into this? I was seventeen when I arrived in New York, an ignorant, backwoods country girl from the deep South, her drawl as distinct as the stars in her eyes, and you know that better than anyone. I thank God every day that Connie Niles saw something in me, or it would have been straight back to Alabama for me. Connie was more than my savior, she was my mentor and my best friend, a sister to me, in those early years."

"And what was I?" Harry growled. "Your sugar daddy?"

"The most daddy I ever knew. He left before I was born, and that's something that's never going to happen to me again. So excuse me for picking my icons carefully."

"Lots of kids don't have fathers," Harry said, his glare harsh and accusing. "How come I've never heard this stuff before? Why didn't you mention this when we were living together?"

Angry, Althea didn't answer. She'd been through all this with Harry before, he just didn't want to admit it. Leaving him had been first and foremost a career decision. Refusing to be baited, she gazed out the window instead, staring absently down at the parking lot where tiny specks of humanity skittered about. She could feel Harry's eyes, feel him waiting for an answer she really didn't have—not anything he'd like to hear, in any case. She had done the unforgivable by asking him to leave, and she wasn't under any illusions that his resentment had faded, even after a decade. When she turned back to him, her face was carefully neutral. Besides, why would she argue with him when he was sick? "Like I said, can we not go there?"

Her retreat annoyed Harry, but he backed off. He would have preferred a battle to her apparent withdrawal, but he didn't have the strength to go there. "Yeah, you're right. It's all a long time ago. So, how has life treated you? Did you ever have any children? I don't recall reading that you did, but I've been away a lot. I might have missed a paper or two." He grinned.

"Children? No, of course not." Althea laughed quietly, surprised at the question.

"'Of course not'?"

"There was never any time."

Her flip tone told Harry that she wasn't telling him the whole story, but he wisely changed the direction of the conversation. "Okay, go on, tell me what happened between you and Connie Niles today."

"There's not much to tell. Connie wasn't very enthusiastic about my asking for work, that's all. As a matter of fact, she turned me down."

Harry was incredulous. "She turned you down? Why? Is the industry in trouble?"

"*I'm* the one in trouble," Althea said softly, her eyes suddenly bleak.

It was worse than bad, it had been humiliating. Her initial reception that morning at the Niles Model Agency had been effusive. Everyone had greeted her warmly, careful to hide their surprise at her unexpected appearance. Not careful enough, though. It was easy to read the questions in their eyes, although they were too polite to ask her anything directly. Fortunately, Connie Niles had ushered Althea into her private office before any embarrassing questions could be posed, and listened carefully while Althea explained.

"I want to come back to work."

Connie had always been a good listener, nothing fazed her. "These men," she clucked sympathetically.

"No, Connie!" Althea had interrupted her quickly. "This is *not* Daniel's fault, nor mine. Things just didn't work out. It will be in all the papers in a few days, when he announces our split, but, please, don't blame him. It was an amicable divorce, I want to be very clear about that. To you most of all, because you've been like a sister to me, and I want you to know how things stand. But don't assign blame where there is none. Like I said, things just didn't work out."

Connie shrugged. "Fine, I won't ask any more questions. Do you have enough money to tide you over?"

"Money is not an issue."

"No, I didn't think so." Never one to mince words, Connie was frank. "Look here, Althea, Ambassador Daniel Boylan is a very popular man—not to mention powerful. And his hailing from New York doesn't help."

"Isn't there anything I can do?"

Connie shrugged her thin shoulders. "You're going to get some mighty bad press—quite dreadful, I would imagine. I can practically write it for you in all its glorious vulgarity. *Black Beauty Abandons Ambassador.* It has a certain ring to it, don't you think?"

"That bad?" Althea sighed.

Connie was emphatic. "You'll make the front pages, for sure, child. But not to worry. It will all die a natural death as soon as the next scandal breaks. There's always another story waiting around the corner. You know that. But until then, darling, until you and Daniel are *not* the story, there's no work for you here in the Big Apple," she said brusquely. "And all that free publicity! What a waste! Too bad, Althea, but you're a bit of a liability now."

Her cheeks burning, Althea had suffered Connie's blunt words. "So you think it's going to be that bad?"

"Well, let me ask you this, sweetie. How do you feel about Los Angeles?"

* * *

"And that was that!" Althea said, as she finished describing the nightmare interview, her eyes flashing. "You would think my name in the papers would please Connie but it seems that Ambassador Daniel Boylan's black shadow hovers over me like a shroud. His stature in the African-American community cannot be 'besmirched'—Connie's word. At least, that's how the agency expects I'm going to be painted when the press gets wind of the story. And because Connie herself is active in the African-American community, she is not going to make waves."

Harry lay there, shaken, unsure what to say. "Divorced? Wow, that's the one thing I never would have guessed. Ah, jeez, Allie, I'm sorry, I really am."

Althea closed her eyes against the sympathy in Harry's voice. "Thanks, but don't be. It was a mutual decision. My first alimony check is already deposited in my bank account and Daniel will continue to make deposits so long as 'I don't cause any scandal.' Real diplomatic of an ambassador, don't you think? The size of the check is his insurance—and it's substantial, to say the least. Not that he can't afford it. Even given that he has the power of his family and the authority of his position to rise above a scandal, he wants to be absolutely certain there won't be any. And that, my friend, is why Connie Niles is not about to risk the wrath of the Boylan family by hiring me."

"They would come after you?"

"With all six barrels blasting." Althea laughed bitterly. "Not that they would find anything. My life is so boring it would please a nun. But the answer is yes, they would come after me. All his life, Daniel has been groomed for big things, and now that he has become a power broker, they aren't going to let anything or anyone spoil it, certainly not an ex-wife. They would look until they found something. Daniel would never know, of course, but a discreet word was dropped in my ear by the family's attorney the day I signed the divorce papers. 'Rumors, my dear, so easily begun, almost impossible to set right....' Don't I know it."

"My God. There's a nasty setup, if ever I heard one. But the Althea Almott I used to know was a pretty tough lady. I can't imagine you taking this lying down. Are you really so worried? The press adores you, if those nasty tabloids I never read are any indication. It's *you* who can't do anything wrong, not Daniel Boylan."

Althea was thoughtful. Her amber eyes, carefully shielded by her long lashes, refused to meet his. "I handled things all wrong."

Some things, in any case. Guilt by omission. Only, she would not share that part of her story. But from day one Daniel believed she had trapped him into marriage with the oldest trick in the book—a pregnancy. As if she'd needed to lower herself to that level. It had been *the press* that had started the rumor, and once begun, it could not be stopped. She had been used to rumors. Models, actors, anyone in the limelight, it was all the same, rumors were always a threat, Daniel should have known that from his own experience. Unfortunately, he seemed not to have thought things out, had mistaken her amusement for confirmation and, diplomat that he was, had never bothered to ask her outright if she was pregnant. Loving him, she had not bothered to deny it. When their marriage was quickly arranged by the Boylan family, she had sat back and let it happen. Okay, a big mistake, but her only one. She had gone along with the marriage because she thought he loved her. He hadn't. It was over the moment he realized that she wasn't pregnant. Courtesy stopped him from requesting a divorce, but his distaste for the situation became untenable. She stayed until she could no longer bear it. Learning that Daniel had not loved her was a wound that would take a long time to heal.

Chapter Four

Harry found himself at cross-purposes. He still harbored enormous anger at Althea for leaving him in the first place, but as she sat by his bedside day after day, making small talk, reading aloud to him, keeping his spirits up, his defenses began to weaken. Since she was now divorced, he didn't have to feel guilty spending time with her. He just wasn't sure he wanted to.

It wasn't as if he hadn't had his heart broken in this lifetime. He'd had two serious—very serious—relationships since Althea, just not serious enough to make a commitment. As a matter of fact, he had met someone right after they broke up, a sweet little thing from Colombia, where he had hidden after their breakup. He still smiled when he recalled the delightful nights they spent on the beach, until her father got wind of their "friendship." In fact, he had been willing to walk down the aisle with her, but she had balked at leaving South America. They were still in negotiations when Harry was felled by his first bout of malaria and headed back to the States. He traveled home alone and didn't worry about returning. She didn't seem to expect him back. In retrospect, he knew he was lucky, that it had been a rebound situation.

Then, three years ago, while doing the college lecture circuit, he had hooked up with a rich college kid from Boston. A one-night stand that turned into a yearlong affair and ended in a fiasco. It seemed she'd forgotten to mention a boyfriend on a European tour.

Now, as he lay in his hospital bed, his body might ache, he could barely keep his food down, and if he sat up too quickly, he was dizzy, but he knew he wasn't entirely miserable. When Althea sat beside him, he was beguiled. She brought books and read quietly, while he drifted in and out of sleep. Another day she surprised him with a radio—he loathed television and refused to rent one. From that day forward, he was able to keep up with the news. She listened patiently when he disparaged the lousy hospital food, and showed up with fresh bread and clear soups. (When the nurses noticed the delicious smells,

Althea arranged to have Chinese take-out delivered to their station.) They discussed her career, and his, the interesting turns they had taken professionally, the places they'd been, the people they had met.

But Harry's favorite thing was to watch how Althea's eyes blazed when he teased her, and he did so every opportunity he got. He liked to watch her tamp down her exasperation when he tried her patience with the silliest demands. He also liked to catch her out, catch her staring when she thought he was sleeping. At such moments he wondered what she was thinking, but he never dared to ask. Other times he pretended to sleep because then she would sit beside him and stroke his brow.

"You seem so rough around the edges," she said one day, while she was combing back his freshly washed hair.

"No evidence of a leavening feminine hand?" he said, his voice ironic.

"Your clothes at the airport… You could use a haircut," she admitted.

"Tell me the truth," he said, sharing her smile, "do you ever have a bad day? Last fall I saw you on the cover of *Ebony*, and I remember wishing I had taken the picture, you looked so beautiful. Then I saw the inside layout, you and your husband hanging out at the embassy—you know, one of those a-day-in-the-life sort of articles—and I was glad I hadn't. Don't get me wrong, I have nothing against the am-

bassador—I don't even know him, just what I read
in the papers—I was just glad I hadn't been there,
that's all. All that connubial bliss would have made
me, um, queasy."

"Well, let that be a lesson," Althea said with a short
laugh, "not to believe everything you read." But before
he could question her curious remark, she smoothly
changed the subject. "Hey, I'm not the only one
who's famous. Have I said how many times I've run
across *your* byline? Harry Bensen Sweeps Himalayas.
Harry Uncovers Hidden Ruins of Hammurabi. Bensen
Photographs Yangtze River. You're as much an ex-
plorer as photographer. I went to one of your exhibits,
you know, the one you had in Paris last fall."

"I wish I'd known. On second thought, I'm glad
I didn't," Harry decided. "I would have been nervous
wondering what you thought of my work."

"Fame *can* be a burden," she said with a stilted
laugh.

Harry was doubtful. "Are you so burdened, Althea? Too pretty, too rich, too many houses?"

Althea looked down at Harry's hands, long, pale
fingers sprinkled with blond hair, handsome hands
that had given her body its first lesson in love. But the
choices they'd made, that she had made the decade
before, were still being played out. If she had regrets,
and she had terrible regrets, she would keep them to
herself. "Let me be, Harry," she said quietly. "Don't
ask me any questions, and I won't ask you mine."

They never got personal again, and they never talked about their past together. Harry would have—it was always a word away from his lips—but Althea's message was clear, and he sensed that one wrong word and she might be out the door, a gamble he didn't want to take.

And he would have touched her—oh, countless times he would have liked to reach out—but his hand always stilled. He would not make the same mistake twice. Her ex-husband, Daniel, was nothing, a year out of Althea's life, a mistake. But wasn't he, too? That's what Harry kept telling himself, the long hours he lay in his hospital bed, up to the very moment he was informed that he could leave the hospital four days later. Very nearly what Althea told herself, too, as she prowled her apartment that long week, so it was not surprising that their needs would blend.

It all played out on her next visit to the hospital. She could hear Harry's voice the moment she left the elevator, heard the chuckling of the nurses as she passed their station. He was sitting up in bed when she entered the room, his hair on end. A young woman was standing at the foot of his bed, clutching a clipboard to her chest, her eyes suspiciously bright.

"I'm sorry you feel that way, Mr. Bensen, but I have to go on record with this."

"You're a bloody social worker, not a psychiatrist.

How old are you, anyway? Fourteen? Fourteen years old and giving me orders? And me old enough to be your father."

The poor young woman was patient, Althea gave her that. Her voice didn't waiver, even if her face was flushed. "Mr. Bensen, I'm not fourteen and I'm not—"

But it was too late. Harry had spotted Althea and decided he had an ally. "Ah, there you are, my dear. Come in, come in. Listen to this, it's a real doozie."

"Mr. Bensen."

But Harry refused to let the social worker say another word, and she was no match for him. There was no way to tame the wrath of Khan. Cautiously, Althea approached his bed, not wishing to become part of the dispute, although she wasn't very hopeful.

"Look what they sent to counsel me," Harry snapped. "A child. A mere babe. And she is insisting that I—"

"Recommended!" the social worker protested. "I only recommended—"

"She only 'recommended,'" Harry mimicked her, his tone scathing, "that I hire a nurse before they discharged me, which they would like to do *yesterday*, if I didn't mind. As if I would mind. And this child here has the nerve to tell me that she is going to arrange everything, as if—"

"Harry, calm down. The whole floor can hear

you." Althea tried to hide her laughter behind a question to the social worker. "Arrange what, miss?"

The social worker was grateful to hear the sympathy in Althea's voice. "I offered to arrange a visiting nurse for Mr. Bensen. The doctors are recommending that Mr. Bensen secure some sort of aftercare until he gets back on his feet, but he doesn't seem to agree," she said sternly.

"The very idea! A stranger in my house…my privacy invaded. It doesn't bear thinking about."

"Harry, would you please let the poor woman talk? She's only trying to help you."

Sensing Althea's support, the young woman ventured a gentle scold. "Yes, Mr. Bensen, please be reasonable. You could hardly feed yourself breakfast this morning, much less bathe or grocery shop. Or…or anything. Not without some help!"

So, there it was, Althea thought, watching Harry sink back into his pillows, worn down by the harsh reality of his ill health. The moment they had crossed paths at Kennedy Airport, Althea had known trouble was brewing. Their history was a path strewn with brutal rejection and cruel words, but here she was, revolving in his orbit, again.

On the other hand, it wasn't as if there was anything else on her horizon. She had been moping all week, feeling sorry for herself, trying far too hard to sort out the jagged pieces of her life. Perhaps this was an opportunity to catch her breath. The past year had wrought such chaos—her husband's disaffection, exile from her beloved Paris. Harry would be a cranky patient, but he would not be unkind, and if there was one thing she needed now, it was a little kindness. No one else was offering it. This morning she had called up four old friends—and got four answering machines.

But was this a risk worth taking? Every look she and Harry shared skirted the ugly past for the sake of Harry's illness, but it lingered, waiting to resurface. Having seen the gleam of despair in his eyes, she had a strong feeling she was about to find out.

"Harry," Althea said with a shake of her head, "why are you putting this woman through such grief? She has a job to do. Let her do it." She peered at the poor girl's identification badge, quivering on her chest. "Miss Farrow, Harry…Mr. Bensen…it was supposed to be a surprise, but…" She glared at Harry. "He's coming home with me. It's all arranged."

Miss Farrow's relief was palpable, and so was Harry's. Pulling a sheath of papers from a folder, Miss Farrow lost no time getting Althea to fill out some questionnaires, while Harry leaned back on his pillow, exhausted. Busy with the social worker, Althea missed the sly look of satisfaction Harry was careful to hide.

The day Harry was discharged, Althea showed up at the hospital wearing a green angora hat, a black parka and blue-and-green mittens.

"Mittens?" Harry teased. "Althea Almott wearing mittens? Is that some sort of fashion statement? What gives? And that parka—I mean, it's okay, but what happened to your fur coat?"

"Sable is too extravagant for Florence Nightingale," Althea explained regally as she threw down her backpack and looked Harry over. She felt relieved to see him dressed, but he looked as though the effort had been exhausting. "Harry, you are the most interesting shade of yellow. Are you sure you're well enough to go home?"

"If we don't leave soon, I won't be responsible for the damage I will do Miss Sparrow—"

"Miss Farrow."

"Whatever. Or any other social worker who tries to walk through that door."

"Okay, okay, don't get all worked up. I've ordered an ambulette, so if you don't mind, I'll go get you checked out. You probably have a slew of prescriptions to fill."

"That I do."

"And you are going to take them all as indicated, with the utmost cooperation, aren't you?" Althea warned as she left the room.

"That I am." Harry smiled to the empty air.

Chapter Five

The couple left Elmhurst Hospital amidst much fan-
fare, Harry having become somewhat of a pet among
the nurses. His pretty-boy looks had sent a message
of helpless appeal, and he had not been above turning on the boyish charm. They would miss Althea,
too, the staff promised as they stopped to say goodbye. It had been fun hanging out with a real celebrity.

Althea had to stifle her laughter the way the
nurses' aides vied to wheel Harry to the elevator,
once she'd packed the last of his things and was
ready to leave. Although another snowstorm was
predicted, it hadn't begun, so the roads remained
plowed. A private ambulette, waiting to drive them

to Althea's apartment, would have no trouble nego-
tiating the roads. It would be a better ride than his
first trip, and Althea could see that Harry was thrilled
to leave the hospital. No doubt he considered the ride
to Manhattan a treat, which she supposed it was,
after being bedridden close to three weeks.

The ambulette drivers insisted on escorting Harry
upstairs in a wheelchair, and the doorman insisted on
helping, too. Having learned who Althea was, the
doorman now treated her with the utmost courtesy. He
couldn't do enough for her—carried her groceries,
took in her packages, delivered her newspaper. Althea
was philosophical about it, allowed him to help, but
it would be a long time before she gave him any tip.

Her apartment was crowded as the ambulette
nurses fell over each other settling Harry into the
guest room. But soon he was tucked between the
fresh sheets of the newly made bed.

Althea had put out a pitcher of water and laid out
fresh towels in the adjoining bathroom. Harry hadn't
noticed. Weak as a kitten, he fell asleep at once and
didn't wake until late that night, when everyone was
long gone. After eating some take-out soup—Althea
never claimed to be a cook—and taking his medicine, he fell back to dreamland, never noticing the
relief on his nurse's apprehensive face. If he kept this
up, Althea thought, she could do this, piece of cake.
But, familiar with Harry Bensen's mercurial temper,
she had a feeling that was wishful thinking.

Harry spent the next few days drinking gallons of hot, sugary tea and eating watery farina, which he swore he would never eat again, once he was on his feet.

Setting his breakfast tray aside, Althea promised that if he showed a modicum of good manners, she might make him something really special for lunch.

"Was that a carrot dangling before him?" Harry asked with a rude glare.

"Mashed potatoes, actually," Althea retorted good-naturedly as she plumped up his pillows. "Mashed potatoes are about my speed, cookingwise. So, do you want me to read to you, or maybe play a game of Scrabble, after that hearty lunch?"

But Harry was feeling uncooperative. He was unused to playing the invalid, and it was beginning to grate on his nerves. If only he weren't so damned weak. "I am sick of being in bed. I am sick of pablum and baby food. I am sick of being sick. I want red meat for dinner, do you understand? A burger or steak, I don't care what it is, as long as it's red. I need to get my blood back."

A finger to her lips, Althea eyed him speculatively. He was getting restless, a good sign. Maybe it *was* time for him to start moving about. "You know, you're right. You need some sort of activity and I know just the thing. I'm going to hire a masseuse for you. There's a woman in the neighborhood I sometimes used. She had magical hands, if I remember correctly."

"Are you nuts?" Harry snorted. "There's no way I'm letting some stranger with greasy hands paw at me. God, what a revolting idea. Who knows where her hands would end up."

"You wish," Althea said, grinning.

"Yeah, I do wish," Harry snapped, itching for a good fight. "You know how long it's been? A whole—"

Laughing, Althea covered her ears with her hands. "Do not go there, Harry Bensen, or you will go straight to a nursing home, I swear."

"Okay, okay, but I am not getting a massage," Harry said adamantly.

Althea lowered her hands. "But, Harry, it's exactly what you need. A blood-pounding workout, and you don't have to lift a finger. I promise you'll feel a hundred percent better. Everyone gets them nowadays. Don't be so old-fashioned."

"Me? I am *not* old-fashioned. I had one once, so there."

"Where was this?"

"I had a massage a few years back, when I was in New Orleans."

"New Orleans?" Althea was contemptuous. "No wonder. I'll bet it was during Mardi Gras, too."

"I was on assignment," Harry protested.

"Yeah, right," Althea snorted. "And were you sober during this assignment, hmm?"

"It was a *great* massage," Harry said, winking.

"Yeah, except it was not a massage, am I right? Okay, I'll get you a male masseur, then."

"Not a chance," Harry said, sliding down beneath his covers. "Unless…unless *you* want to do it," he suggested, his blue eyes twinkling as he raised himself up on one elbow. "I'd let *you* give me a massage. Right now, if you like."

Althea met his infectious grin with her own as she pushed him back down against the pillows. "Okay, tough guy, I'll tell you what. *I'll* give a you massage—a real massage—if you let me call in a barber."

"Ooh, my hair, now you want to cut my hair? Why does everyone always wants to cut my hair? Who do you think I am, Samson?"

Ignoring his lamentations, Althea continued to negotiate. "Come on, what do you say? In a week or so, when you are feeling a little stronger. Quite frankly, Harry, you're looking more like Rapunzel than Samson, these days."

"Oh, I am *so* not amused."

"Oh, and I am *so* going to get the baby oil," she mimicked as she disappeared into the bathroom. "And you are *so* going to do what I say."

Harry grinned with pure satisfaction as Althea banged the cabinet doors open and shut, looking for some oil. Never underestimate the power of your opponent, he thought with a lazy smile. His body was tingling with anticipation, and she hadn't even begun.

He would have to be cool, though. If he were cool, he bet he could wrangle a massage from Althea *every* day.

Holding a bottle of baby oil aloft, she emerged from the bathroom. "Success."

Harry contrived to look as weak as possible without destroying his chance of success. He sucked in his cheeks and fluttered his eyes. "Shirt off," he heard her command. This, he thought, is what is meant by to die and go to Heaven.

Harry cooperated as best he could, he really tried, but he simply could not manage the buttons.

"Allow me," Althea said, brushing aside his shaking hands. Sitting beside him, she began to open his pajama buttons as he lay back against the pillows, too weak to stir. With every button twist, she expected his scrawny chest to appear, lily-white and undernourished.

Except that he wasn't lily-white, Althea groaned to herself as she spread apart his shirt. South American sun had seen to that.

And he was definitely not undernourished. The strong, hard planes of his chest attested to that. Actually, he was what her personal trainer might call "sculpted." A gift from God, because if there was one thing she knew about Harry Bensen, he had never seen the inside of a gym.

And that thick mat of brown hair covering his chest, she didn't remember *that*. Good grief. How was she going to manage a massage when her hands wanted to play?

"Harry, turn over." She could not possibly begin with his chest.

The cottony smell of freshly laundered linen mingled with Harry's own distinct healthy male scent as she helped him remove his pajama top. Balancing his weight was precarious business. He seemed a bit dizzy the way he kept falling into her arms. Eventually, though, she managed to slide one sleeve off. No wonder she was having trouble. His arms were so muscular he probably needed a bigger size of pajama.

Helping Harry to turn onto his belly, she was doubly alarmed how his muscles rippled as he tucked his hands beneath the pillow. The way she blushed, she was glad he wasn't facing her. Pouring a few drops of oil in her hands, she rubbed her palms together to remove the chill.

"Althea, you still there?"

"I, um…"

Her mouth too dry to speak, Althea felt her face grow hot and she prayed he didn't hear the quaver in her voice. The way her heart was thumping, she wouldn't be surprised he could hear that. Cautiously she placed her quivering hands on his brawny shoulders, barely able to span the breadth of his well-honed back. Slowly she began to knead his shoulders, his skin smooth and supple beneath her fingers.

Touching him this way brought back memories, and she was glad he couldn't see her face. He would too easily read the embarrassment in her eyes. She almost lost track of her purpose, as thirty minutes flew by. Noticing his eyes closed, she hoped he was falling asleep.

Her fingers worked their magic across his back and down his spine, inching back up his waist. Recalling how ill he'd been, she marveled that he'd even had the strength to make it home to New York.

"Harry, what on earth were you thinking to travel back from Brazil alone in this condition?"

"I had no one to call," Harry murmured, as he fell asleep. "Until you…"

Surprised and confused, Althea stood staring down at her patient, then quietly slipped from the bedroom. She was unaware of the blue eyes that followed her, suddenly alert and filled with uncertain longing.

Chapter Six

Fancy food at fancy prices, Althea thought wryly as she browsed the aisles of D'Agostino's Supermarket a week later, searching out specialties to tempt Harry's appetite. Not a blueberry to be had, either, unless one counted the frozen kind. Maybe she should try a high-end gourmet food emporium like Zabar's, but she was in a lazy mood and didn't want to walk. Finally she settled on fresh string beans, a rotisserie chicken and genuine English clotted cream, into which she would fold some fresh strawberries. If that didn't put the pounds back on Harry Bensen, nothing would. Not that he wasn't gaining weight. She knew this for a fact. His morning rubdown bore this out. Every workout told her that he was becoming healthier.

The happy invalid was sitting in the kitchen, nursing a cup of green tea and honey when she walked through the door and plopped her brown D'Ag bags on the table.

"Why, Harry, you're up."

Harry fastened his mocking eyes on hers. "Yes, I do believe I am. I was just having some tea. Vile stuff, green tea. What took you so long?"

"Is that your way of saying you missed me?" Althea laughed as she shrugged off her parka.

"He had me for company, but I think we're talking apples and oranges," said Leonel, as he strode into the kitchen carrying a stack of photographs.

"Leonel!"

"Uh-oh. By the surprise on your face, I'd guess that Harry forgot to mention I was stopping by."

"Harry's not too good at those kinds of details."

"Sorry, Allie, I forgot that Leonel was coming."

"Not at all. You're always welcome here, Leonel. Let me put these groceries away and I'll leave you two alone."

"No, wait. Don't go," Harry protested. "You've got so much experience with photography, it shouldn't go to waste."

"Why, that's right kindly of you, Harry," Althea teased. "But I have things of my own to do."

"I hate to say it, Althea, but for once Harry's

right," Leonel agreed. "Come on into the dining room for a minute and see what our boy here has brought back from Brazil. The man's a positive genius with a Nikon."

Althea followed the men into the next room to find the dining room table covered with Harry's photographs. In silence she circled the table, while Leonel added more from a box on the floor, and Harry dodged her footsteps.

"That's Manaus, the small town on the Amazon that I told you about. It was my base of operations, I think I mentioned. Pretty little place. Oh, and that one's an overview of the rainforest, thirty miles downriver."

Every step she took, Harry gave a running commentary, and she could tell he was proud of his work.

"Harry, these are gorgeous. Look at this," she said, lifting a photo of a deep-purple orchid growing on a thick branch. "It's exquisite. But how did you get up so high? Oh, Harry, tell me that you didn't climb this tree. Leonel, does this mean you're going to submit his work for a Pulitzer?" Althea asked as she pored over the pictures.

"I most certainly am. The application is due in February, and that's one deadline I'm going to see my client here doesn't miss. To tell the truth, if Harry wasn't so good, I wouldn't bother, but he *is* good, so he gets a lot of TLC. He does make the company lots of money," Leonel added.

"Leonel, you just enjoy bullying a sick man," Harry protested, but Althea could see that he was pleased.

"Harry, that's wonderful." On impulse she kissed his cheek, surprising them both. Her cheeks burning, Althea backed away. "Well then, I guess I'll leave you two alone. I have my own list of chores to complete, nothing as enjoyable as this, though." With a last admiring glance at the photos, she left the room.

Silently, Harry and Leonel leaned over the dining room table and began to sort the pictures into various categories. But Harry's newfound concentration didn't fool Leonel. For one thing, his cheeks were still red, and for another, he was making a mess of the pictures. Shuffling the pile of photographs in his hand, Leonel smiled. "My, my, Harry, one little kiss and you fall apart."

"No such thing," Harry protested. "But, hey, listen, Leonel. Althea's been a little testy the past few days. Cabin fever, I guess. Do me a favor. Take her out for some fresh air."

"But she just came home."

"I mean to dinner or something. I'm sort of housebound, and she's used to the nightlife."

"And just how would you know that? You said you hadn't seen each other in years, until you swept her off her feet at the airport. Or, oh, pardon me, it was the other way round, wasn't it?"

"Very funny. But you get the idea."

"Harry." Leonel chuckled. "You sure have a strange way of courting a woman."

"I'm doing no such thing."

"Yeah, right. Then are you saying that Miss Almott is fair game? Because if you are, a fine black man like me is a great catch for a fine black woman like Althea. I've been thinking of settling down, having kids, buying a house. I've been looking at some real estate in New Jersey, down by the shore. All right, maybe not the Jersey shore," he said, laughing at the look on Harry's face. "But somewhere. The pleasure of coming home to a home-cooked meal has been on my mind lately."

"Oh, jeez, talk about courting, you going to tell that to Althea? She doesn't cook worth a dime, I can tell you right now, and somehow I don't think that's the direction to take with her. She's got her own ideas about how her life should go, and getting married is not high on the list, from what I've observed. And, anyway, why does the future Mrs. Murray have to be black? You one of those that sticks to your own kind?" Harry snorted. "Althea is sure going to appreciate your loving her for herself. No need to let a little something like love interfere."

"I'm sure she would engage my, er, passion, eventually."

"Come over here, Leonel, and put your cheek on my fist. I'm too weak to punch you out without some help."

Leonel leaned forward, dangling his hands between his knees, his face suddenly thoughtful as he chose his words carefully. "You don't care for my brand of honesty, Harry? My mistake. I didn't say the woman I married *had* to be black, but I do have to admit that I try to avoid crossing the color line whenever I can. *Because I don't want to!* There are too many problems in a mixed marriage, for my taste. The looks you get walking down the street, too many restaurant tables by the kitchen, silly family stuff, like Thanksgiving dinner, for instance. Now, *that* could be interesting. And the kids, how about the kids, not sure which side of the fence to sit on. Me, I'm not sure what I'd tell them. I can't explain it better than that, except to add that it sure wouldn't thrill my mother."

"How can you control that sort of thing? The heart goes where it goes."

Leonel spread his hands. "Okay, say for argument's sake that I fell in love with a white woman. Well, that would be that. I'm simply saying that I would prefer that not to happen, and I do my best not to be in a position to test myself. That's how it is for me. I would be proud of what I was, whatever I was, I just happen to be black. If that's the route *you* want to take, though, that's your choice. But, Harry, if you think it's nobody's business, guess again. It's *everybody's* business. They make it so."

"Starting here?" Harry asked wryly.

"Listen up, my friend. If you think you'd sail through life married to a black woman, forget about it. But you must know that already."

Harry was thoughtful as he scratched at his five-o'clock shadow. "I'm pretty sure that's why Althea dumped me, way back when. She's pretty much said so, that she was pressured by her friends."

Leonel was philosophical. "Maybe her best friends, and maybe the best advice she ever got."

"You think so? Hell, Leonel, you sure don't mince words, do you? It's a running argument between us. I say that she didn't stand up for us, and she says that she was too young to make such a big decision. Maybe she was, but the way I figure things, if you want something badly enough, you go after it."

Leonel's laugh was full and unconditional. This was nothing he hadn't heard before. "You say that because you're a man, and a white man, to boot. White men don't always see the bigger picture, my friend. They don't have to."

"You playing the race card, Leonel?"

"Ah, yes, *ye olde race card.* Look, Harry, I'm not saying you don't understand race as an intellectual issue. You just don't live with it, is all, and there's a world of difference. If you and Althea hooked up, you would be singing a different song. It's nothing personal, I know you try to understand, I know the life you lead is a reflection—or a result, if you will—of your conscience, and your conscientiousness. I'm simply telling you the way things are. You can believe me or not."

Harry's eyes flickered with annoyance. "I'm not going to argue with you, because I happen to think you're right, and isn't that the whole thing in a nutshell? I would like to be with Althea—there, I admit it—but I don't think she wants to go the extra mile you're talking about."

Leonel responded to the apprehension in Harry's voice with only a hint of indignation because he loved Harry and Harry had always been a good friend to him. His blunt words were a reflection of his own frustrations. "Well, Harry, can you blame her? Have you thought what her life would be like if she married a white guy? Don't you think she has more to lose than you do? You think the white community is narrow-minded, the sisterhood is a *very* tight-knit community and does not take kindly to mixed marriage. Almost two-thirds of mixed marriages in the African-American community are between a *black* man and a *white* woman, *not* the other way round. Now, why do you think that is, my fine young Viking?"

"Leonel, I'll be damned if I am going to take responsibility for everything that's wrong with the world. I used to be in love with Althea. And I thought there was no one or nothing that could cheat us of a life together."

"Except Althea."

"Except Althea. She didn't want to meet me half-way, and I respected her wishes."

"Harry, haven't you been listening to me?" Leonel snapped. "For a black woman, the distance she walks is more than halfway, it's probably closer to two damned thirds. And if we want to be truthful, it spreads beyond marriage. The black community is a matriarchal society, remember? It goes for her family, which the black woman pretty much raises without a husband, to her job. So, if Althea is fearful, don't blame her entirely. Life is not that simple. Not for black women. Not for *any* woman, no matter her skin color, who raises her children single-handedly."

"But you forgot one thing, Leonel. It's got to change sometime."

Leonel nodded. "True enough. *When* is the question. Okay, Harry, you have my support, no matter what."

"Thanks. But the question is," Harry asked with a flash of humor, "would you dine with me and Althea at all those fancy restaurants you were talking about before?"

"Oh, yeah." Leonel grinned. "I'm going to sit with you and Althea—right next to that swinging kitchen door!"

"Good. When that happens we can discuss the existential symbolism of seating plans."

"Oh, right," Leonel growled. "Like you never heard of Rosa Parks?"

Hearing the sound of their deep male laughter,

Althea was just about to investigate when the doorbell rang. Her surprise gave way to pleasure as she opened the door to see Benicia Ericson standing in the hall, a cautious look in her eyes.

"Hi. You did say to come by anytime. I was in the neighborhood, so I thought I'd stop by for a minute. Are you busy?"

Althea welcomed Benicia with a warm hug. "No, I'm not busy," she said as she ushered Benicia in. "I'm glad you made the time."

"Wow. What an incredible place you have," Benicia said, agog at the pink marble flooring, the delicate wall sconces decorating the etched wallpaper, and the fresh flowers filling the crystal vases. Spotting a display of photographs along the far wall, she couldn't help her curiosity.

"Go ahead and look." Althea smiled as she took Benicia's coat. "That's why I hung them up. People were always asking me to show them some pictures and I got tired of pulling out the albums."

Althea had had an amazing career, as the photographs attested. *Cover Girl, Ebony, W, Vanity Fair.* Althea's beautiful face had appeared on the covers of all the big-name magazines, and there were countless commercial photographs, too, and then the less formal portraits, taken by friends. But no pictures of Althea's ex-husband.

"You didn't bring your son," Althea observed as she hung Benicia's coat in the closet.

"I can tell you don't have kids." Benicia smiled. "James is in school. He's in the first grade."

"Oh, right. Then you'll bring him next time, promise? Still, I'm glad you stopped by. Didn't you think I was serious when I invited you?"

"I wasn't sure," Benicia confessed as she studied a black-and-white montage. "I had a meeting in the neighborhood, and I remembered you lived hereabouts. I got to thinking that it might be nice to stay in touch with a friend from home. I lost a lot of friends. My family, too. Everyone fell by the wayside when I left Alabama. It was very hard—the hardest thing I've ever done—leaving home like that. But I will say this, I chose to come to New York because of you, Althea. I figured if little Althea Almott could do it, so could I. God takes care of fools." She laughed as she walked with Althea to the living room.

"But why didn't you call me? Why didn't you ever let me know you were here?"

"Hey, listen, I wasn't here for a career move, honey. I was pregnant. And you're forgetting that we weren't what you call *good* friends when you left. We'd had a big fight, if you remember? Look, I can say it now, I was jealous. Oh, wow, will you look at this living room! It's gorgeous, Althea, just gorgeous."

Althea looked around, trying to see the room through Benicia's eyes. The satiny reflection of the long yellow silk drapes, parted to allow the afternoon sun to filter through the French doors, gave the room a rich glow. Favoring simple lines, Althea had decorated with a light hand. It allowed the living room to retain an uncluttered look even though there was plenty of furniture scattered about. Two sofas done in pale-yellow silk were piled high with brocade pillows. A gray carpet ran wall to wall. Colorful rugs were scattered about to offset the look. The overall sense was of comfort and good taste.

"Did you decorate it yourself?"

Althea nodded. "It took some time, what with working and traveling, but I've been here for years, so it didn't matter. I did what I could when I could."

"It's lovely, truly lovely. Hey, do you really not mind my being here? You're so rich and famous, you're almost like a movie star. I don't know what I was thinking, stopping by. It's only for a few minutes, I promise. I'm sure you have tons of things to do and you're just being nice."

"Benicia, you're making me nervous. I invited you, didn't I?"

"But looking at you—so pretty and all, and this fancy apartment. Yes, I'm definitely out of my league."

"Benicia."

Benicia laughed as she sank into a lush sofa, her brown eyes twinkling. "All right, I love it, I admit it. I feel like a queen and I'm totally jealous. But I'll try not to let it spoil my visit, I promise."

Althea shook her head with a smile. "Thank you. I was wondering. Now, would you like some tea?"

"No, I really do only have about twenty minutes before I have to get back uptown."

"You know, you never did say what you did for a living."

"Didn't I?" Benicia said, tearing her eyes from a delicate antique clock resting on the mantel. "I'm the director of the Bronx Home for Unwed Mothers. A natural evolution, you might say," she said with a grin.

"I'm impressed."

"You're nice to say so, but don't be. Oh, it's a great job and I love my girls, but I got it partly because I came up through the ranks, so to speak, and I sure don't want credit for that! Looking back, I'm surprised I even survived. It was dumb luck, if you want to know the truth."

"What happened? How did you live when you got here?" Althea asked, curious to hear Benicia's story.

"I lived on the streets, like most runaways. I had secretly saved up some money, and James's daddy gave me a few dollars. I had about a hundred dollars in my pocket, so I figured I wouldn't starve, right off. Lordy, I thought I was a millionaire with all that cash! Heaven knows what I thought was going to happen when my money ran out. Most kids don't think that far ahead, that's why the subways are of full of runaways. When the money runs out, it's a warm place to go. Nobody goes to the shelters unless they're forced by the cops. Me, I rode the trains and panhandled, washed up best I could in public rest rooms. I thank God to this very day that I wasn't hurt or worse. I lasted three weeks until a Good Samaritan found me. She later said it was the absolute look of terror on my face that drew her to me. It sure wasn't the way I smelled." Benicia grinned.

"You're laughing. I'm shocked."

"Oh, yeah. I can laugh now, but I sure wasn't laughing then. Anyway, my savior's name was Tami Leuong. She was the director of a girls' home up in the Bronx, and she dragged me up there. The first thing Tami did was feed me, then she put me to bed. Didn't even make me take a bath until the next day, bless her heart. But after that shower, we had a long, long talk. Tami Leuong saved my life, Althea, and my son's. I had my baby and ended up living there for six years while I got my GED. Then I went on to a community college, and when the time came to get a job, Tami was about to retire. It was a no-brainer. I'm just giving back a little of what was given to me. But the pleasure's all mine, as the saying goes."

Althea blinked rapidly, hoping Benicia wouldn't notice her tears. "I don't know what to say."

"You may think I wasn't so lucky, Althea, but I was. Some girls aren't. Some girls never get off that train, you know what I mean? Those that do, I help them make their own luck. And as for my baby, I have no regrets. James is the best thing that ever happened to me. He made me turn myself around."

Althea's eyes clouded with nightmarish visions of what it must have been like for Benicia, alone in the big, cold city, a city so unlike Birmingham, so far from the warmth of the South.

"I do have to admit, though," Benicia said, continuing her nightmare journey, "that being a single mom is not where I thought I was heading, when I was a kid. I had dreams, too. Not as grand as yours, of course," Benicia said, aware of the wealth that surrounded her. She knew full well that Althea's designer clothes didn't come from the local clothes rack, that her red leather shoes were handmade, and Benicia didn't doubt for a moment that those were originals hanging on the walls. But the look she sent Althea was tender.

"We sure didn't follow the same career path, did we?" she said with a shy tilt of her head.

"But you have a son," Althea said, her voice a hoarse mix of emotions.

"I have a son. But enough of me. What about you, Althea? How was it for you, coming to New York with about as little money as I had, I'd guess, and knowing not much more? And I'm not talking about the party line—you know the stuff they print in the papers about you, although I don't mean to pry. I'm just asking as an old friend, curious as to how it went the first day, the first year." Sweeping the beautiful room with her eyes, Benicia had to smile. "I'm guessing you didn't sleep on the subways."

Althea was thoughtful as she forced herself to look back, something she tried to avoid at all cost. So many mistakes, she thought to herself, but no, never a night on the subway. "I had an auntie here, although to this day I'm not sure she really was. My mother was never clear about that, but she sent me to live with Auntie Jean and that gave me a roof over my head. And my mother gave me one year to prove myself. Between the two of them, I was safe."

"Safe from what?"

"Well, drugs for one. A lot of bad stuff goes on in the big city. Auntie Jean protected me from that. Set me a strict curfew, first thing, I think it was eight o'clock," Althea said with a laugh. "And then I met my agent, Connie Niles, and she protected me, too. I must have had the word *innocent* written on my forehead, the way everybody took care of me. Even the other models I met were careful not to…corrupt me. I remember once I tried to smoke a cigarette and, boy, did I catch hell. From Iman herself! Strolled right up to me—just imagine, a million-dollar model like Iman caring about a little nobody like *me*—grabbed the cigarette right out of my mouth and read me the riot act. Went on for ten minutes about cancer and the stink and how uncool it was to smoke. Of course, it helped that she threatened to tell my momma."

"You got lucky."

"Very lucky, and don't I know it." It only turned sour later on, Althea reflected. The mess she'd made of her personal life—with her ex-husband and Harry Bensen—far outweighed any other problems she had faced. But she would not share that with anyone.

"Benicia, can you—" But whatever Althea was going to ask was lost in the shuffling of footsteps. They turned just in time to see Harry cross the threshold, his bedroom slippers making a scuffing sound.

"Allie, honey," he said, holding a photograph, "Leonel wants to know what you think of this—" The look of surprise on Benicia's face was no less wary than Harry's. "Sorry, I didn't know you had company."

"Neither did I," Benicia apologized as she scrambled to her feet.

The embarrassment on Benicia's face at the sight of a strange man wandering around in beat-up dungarees and a T-shirt told Althea and Harry both what she was thinking. "Althea, you should have mentioned you had company."

"Harry's not company," Althea explained quickly. "He was just discharged from the hospital and had nowhere to go. He's my patient, sort of." She laughed. "But don't worry, he's not contagious."

"Depends on what you want to catch," Harry teased as he plopped down on the couch. "A bacterial virus, actually," Harry explained with a quick smile.

Even his disease seemed exotic to Benicia. "That sounds serious. But you don't look all that sick," she added, her voice a shade skeptical.

Althea followed Benicia's eyes. Harry *was* looking better, now that she mentioned it. There even seemed to be a tinge of pink to his cheeks. His unshaven cheek... It was time for that haircut; she made a mental note to call her hairdresser. And maybe pick him up a new pair of jeans. No need to show off his knees like that. "Benicia Ericson, meet Harry Bensen. Harry, meet an old friend of mine from Alabama."

"Not that old," he said politely, leaning forward to shake hands with Benicia.

"Okay, you got me. Flattery will get you everywhere." Benicia laughed softly as she sat back down. "But I'll bet you knew that."

"Watch out, ma'am," a deep voice said. "He's fast and he's good, but kept men are notoriously expensive."

"Yo, Leonel," Harry beckoned, "come meet Althea's friend, Benicia Ericson. Benicia, meet Leonel Murray, my editor."

"Editor and friend," Leonel elaborated, extending his hand to Benicia. "The editor in me helps Harry to put his books together. The friend in me helps Harry to put Harry together."

"And that drawl puts your roots somewhere… south."

"You say south like it's a dirty word, Miss Ericson."

"As a child of the south, I know whereof I speak. It's a hard place to grow up. I have my prejudices," she said with a small smile.

Leonel looked at her for a minute, then burst out laughing. "And not far from the surface, I see."

Benicia's eyes twinkled. "Yeah, I guess. But they could be worse."

"I suppose. And how far do these prejudices extend? Not to New York, I hope?"

Surprised by his question, Benicia looked to Althea for guidance, unsure if Leonel was being flirtatious. It was Harry who lightened the moment with his own dry wit.

"Pay no attention, Benicia. A certain editor thinks he is God's gift to journalism, so please forgive Leonel his impudence. Or is it imprudence? I can never tell."

"Harry is a photojournalist," Althea explained to Benicia's confusion.

"That's pretty impressive. I love to look at old photographs. They are so poignant. Like looking in somebody's window, almost."

"I don't do quite that kind of work, but if you like, I can send you and your family tickets to my next exhibit. It's sometime in June."

"That would be wonderful. Two are enough, it's

just me and my son, and he'll be thrilled. Speaking of which, school is out in less than an hour," she said, glancing at her watch, "which means that I have a bus to catch."

"Can I drop you anywhere?" Leonel asked, rising with her. "I've got to get back to work and my car is right outside."

"Where are you headed? I'm going uptown."

"What a coincidence," Leonel said quickly. "I'm going that way, too."

Chapter Seven

Closing the door on her visitors, Althea headed for the kitchen. Shaking his head, Harry followed behind.

"Did you see that? Did you see the way he was behaving?" he asked, incredulous.

Carrots, celery, an onion. How could anyone mess up a pot of soup? she thought. Water, vegetables and salt, wasn't that it? She wondered if her mamma was home.

"The way who was acting?" she asked, only half listening as she started pulling vegetables from the refrigerator.

"Leonel," Harry said, sounding exasperated by her inattention. Was she really going to cook?

. "The way he was bowled over by your girlfriend, helping her on with her coat, offering to drive her uptown. His office is five blocks away, for Pete's sake. It seemed a bit much, didn't you think?"

Althea straightened up, her hands so full of vegetables she almost didn't make it to the kitchen sink. "Is there something wrong with being nice to a lady?"

"That's not what I meant. It's just that he told me less than an hour ago that he was looking to get married. Now he's hitting on a woman he hasn't known even ten minutes."

"Then you're saying that you don't believe in love at first sight?" Althea said as she began to wash the vegetables.

"Not relevant."

"To you maybe, but it seems it is to Leonel. If he is attracted to Benicia then what's wrong with a little investigative reporting? Driving her home, I mean."

"But don't you think he ought to get to know her better?"

"How is he going to do that? Wait to bump into her here? Come on, Harry, it's harmless."

Harry wasn't satisfied, but since Althea refused to see his point of view, he dropped the subject. Together, they cleaned vegetables in companionable silence, although Althea did the cutting while Harry watched. He might not be sure how her soup was going to turn out, but he sure liked watching the way she moved around the counter, liked the sway of her hips as she bent over the cutting board. Steps away from making a fool of himself, he forced himself to sit down. He would not seduce her in her own home, where she trusted him to behave. But watching the way her sweater brushed against her breast, he allowed himself to fantasize.

In a fantasy, he could tiptoe up behind her and wrap his arms about her waist. He could imagine her laughter, her look of surprise that didn't quite say *stop*. He could slip his hands beneath her pretty cashmere sweater and press his palms against her midriff. He could slide his fingers along her smooth, brown skin, cup her breast, stroke her ever so lightly. Her nipples would pucker, she would want him to touch her again, but he would make her wait, maybe nuzzle her soft neck as he pulled her against his body. Then he would plant tantalizing kisses along a slow path to her mouth as he turned her in his arms.

He watched her lips close over the silver spoon as she tested the flavor of the soup. He watched her turn to him and smile. "Ah, jeez, I can't stand this," he muttered, and, rising abruptly, hurried from the kitchen.

Alarmed, Althea followed him into the living room. "Harry, what's wrong? Are you feeling all right? You looked so pale suddenly."

Harry drew a hand down over his face and across

his chin. He stared at Althea, impatient and unsure what to say. The depth of his feelings leaped like electricity across the small space between them, but her understanding was instant. Suddenly it was easy for her to see the emotion coiled within him, to understand the meaning of his clenched hands, the reason he lowered his eyes. The way he framed his question was soft and tender, almost a whisper. "What are we going to do about this, Althea?"

Althea didn't pretend to misunderstand his meaning, but she didn't have an answer. And she didn't want to discuss it. The attraction that was drawing her to Harry Bensen was something she wasn't ready to confront. She would think it over when she was alone. Now that she knew he felt the same way, she wasn't sure how to proceed. If in the end she decided to pursue a relationship, she wanted to be a willing participant, in control of the direction she would take. She did not want to be seduced.

But she didn't mind being kissed. When he cupped her face between his long fingers and pulled her close, she made no objection.

Harry would never say he hadn't been kissed in his lifetime, but he would say he had never been kissed like this before. The Althea he had kissed ten years ago had been sweet but childlike. The kiss he stole from her now was the kiss of a grown woman. When he pressed his mouth to hers, he found he couldn't leave. His greedy mouth meant to only stay a moment, brush a path through her resistance to some sort of response. *Something! Anything!* So that he was stunned to feel her soft lips return his kiss, create a disturbance he had not felt in years.

Lifting his mouth, he ran his thumb across her delicate jaw. "You must know that I want you, right?"

"I did guess something of the sort," Althea said softly, her eyes closing against the sensations caused by the simple touch of this man. Familiar, total and involuntary.

"Then you must know that keeping my hands to myself is beginning to prove impossible."

Althea opened her eyes, her amusement deep. "But, Harry, do you have the strength for this?"

Silly question. Over and over, he kissed her mouth, the hollow at the base of her throat, brushed her forehead with his lips, brushed her temple until she was giddy. "Stop. Stop," she said, lauging, "I can't breathe."

Sweeping her into his arms, Harry deepened the kiss as they moved together to a new level. At first gentle, then searching, his kisses triggered a spiral of sensation within Althea. She couldn't help but wrap her arms about his neck, bow into his hard body. He was so enticing. Her hands crept beneath his T-shirt of their own volition, to span the plane of his back, knead the hot, dry skin that met her palms. Parting her lips, Althea met his mouth with her own desire. How *had* they made it this far without touching?

Harry's embrace was timid as he drew her into the circle of his arms. One arm around her waist, the other at the small of her back, he clasped her firmly as they tried for some semblance of control. Her face tucked against his chest, Althea felt his uneven breathing. His clean, male scent was transfixing, his strong arms suddenly a safety net, and she gave herself over to the comfort of his arms…

…until the soup boiled over, and they stepped back, suddenly embarrassed, the moment lost to more earthly matters.

The news of Althea's divorce hit the newsstands faster than she expected. Apparently she had been spotted by some rogue reporter who had done his homework and fed the news to an entertainment weekly. When Althea tried to run an errand the next morning, the doorman stopped her as she exited the elevator. "Miss Almott, ma'am?"

Althea heard the warning in his voice and followed his hand as he pointed to the lobby door. "Oh, no."

His quick thinking saved her huge embarrassment. Outside on the sidewalk, she could see a small band of reporters milling about, trying unsuccessfully to warm themselves with steaming cups of coffee. Microphones clutched tightly in their gloved hands, they waited for their story, and apparently she was it. Quickly she stepped back and sped upstairs to announce the news to Harry.

"It was only a matter of time," he said. "Perhaps less than you'd hoped for, but no big surprise when you think about it. It's not like this hasn't happened before, is it? What you *do* about it is the main concern. Do you want to leave the city, go upstate, leave the country, maybe? I have friends in foreign places. Oh, but you do, too, I forgot. Well, it's your call."

Harry watched as Althea thought about her options, curled up on the sofa, her chin resting on her knees. She looked so bereft he would have liked to sit beside her and give her a supportive hug. He would have liked to wrap his arms about her shoulders and promise her that everything would be all right. Maybe plant a kiss in her hair, tease a smile from her. He would have liked to take liberties, but he was careful not to. She was coltish and he didn't want to frighten her. "Can't you go home? Your mother would give you shelter, wouldn't she?"

"Of course she would," Althea said in a huff, "but I'd hate to do that to her, even though she's dealt with reporters before. And go back to Alabama? I don't know. That's the first place they'd look, don't you think? In fact, they may be camped out on her doorstep even as we speak. I'd better call and see how she's doing."

Harry shook his head as Althea reached for the

phone. "I don't think it's that urgent. Don't you think she would have called if they were there? Why would they bother flying down south when they know you're here in New York?"

"That's true." Althea fell back against the cushions, unsure what to do. She hated leaving her pretty apartment, especially when she had just moved back. She liked the cheerful yellows that made her feel as if she'd captured sunshine, even on a rainy day. She liked her well-equipped kitchen. Even if she couldn't cook, she had been hoping to learn. She especially liked crawling into bed at night with a good book, her down duvet floating around her. The routine she had begun to establish was a carefully constructed shield, a comfort zone she was trying to create against the ferocious pain of her divorce. Her life had about-faced so suddenly she didn't want another turnabout, even if it was necessary to her well-being and safety.

Harry might not know the specifics but, watching her face take on a host of emotions, he intuitively knew her worries and wanted to help. He only wished his suggestions didn't sound so thin. "Connie won't help you, she's already told you what a liability you are, but what about Benicia?"

Althea looked away. "I don't want to ask her."

He was surprised but when Althea explained her reluctance, he understood.

"Now that we've renewed our friendship, I don't want to ask her any favors. Besides, she's got her hands full with her son, James, remember? She wouldn't appreciate the notoriety any more than my mother, I'm sure."

"You may be right. I wouldn't, in her place. And it might not be the safest situation, either, for the kid. Well then, I guess the ball is in my court."

"The ball is in your court?" Althea echoed.

"I have a house in Brooklyn," he revealed quietly. "We'd be safe there for a while."

Althea was on him in a second. "You have a house in Brooklyn and you never said?"

"Hey, calm down, sweetie. My dusty mansion hasn't been occupied in ages. Unlike a certain wealthy woman who shall go unnamed, *I* cannot afford a housekeeper. As a matter of fact, it's under renovation."

"Then how can you offer it up?"

"Because a third of the house was completed the last time I checked, significant parts like the bedrooms and bath. I didn't furnish it much, but it's definitely habitable. If my contractors haven't lied to me, they're in the homestretch. I think there's only the kitchen left, and that shouldn't be a problem because we can order in food. Before I left for South America, they had laid most of the new flooring, on the second floor, at least. Someday, I'm going to have a huge master bath installed right next to my bedroom. And if you're worrying about having your own bedroom, you can have your choice of three. But that includes mine," he said with a grin.

"Harry!"

"Hey, you never know. Yeah, I guess I do," he said, seeing her frown. "Aw shucks, ma'am, you know darn well I'm still in the invalid stage. Or is that wishful thinking?"

"Harry!"

"Just kidding. Come on, Allie, you're as pretty as a picture. A man can dream, can't he?"

"Not when he's inviting me into his web," she said, her lips pursed.

"Have it your way," Harry sighed. "But just so you know, the living room is habitable, even by your standards. Maybe not as fancy as this place," he said, looking around him, "but comfy enough."

"So that leaves—?"

"Mostly the kitchen. But that's not something that would concern you, is it?" Harry asked with a wry laugh.

Althea wasn't sure. "I do like my coffee. How bad is it?"

"Come on, Allie, I'm offering you sanctuary. We'll have a good time, I promise. There are tons of restaurants in the area, and I've even noticed a spa or two. We'll manage."

"*We?*"

"I can't let you go alone, can I?" Harry said smoothly. "Look at it as my way of saying thank you, Allie. Go with it, it's pretty rare."

Althea was of two minds about what to do but

saved from making a decision when the doorbell rang. It was Leonel, dashing past Althea when she opened the door, bringing more than the cold air with him.

"Have you seen today's papers?" It was a moot point. "Pick any," he said, dropping a bundle on the coffee table. "You've made the front page, Althea. You and your ex-husband. You guys have a problem. Althea does, anyway, if that crowd of reporters downstairs is any indication."

Crouching down on her knees, Althea spread the papers out. *Althea Abandons Ambassador. Model Mayhem.* She read each headline with mounting horror. "I think I'm open to suggestions."

Chapter Eight

Leaving Althea's apartment building had been easy. Only the tenants and the building staff were privy to the existence of the secret door hidden in the boiler room, which led to the alleyway. That hidden door was the reason for the exorbitant rent they all willingly paid, and many a tenant had made use of it. Harry and Althea slipped through the door, thankfully, and were relieved to see Leonel parked steps away. Carefully following Harry's direction, they were soon driving over the Brooklyn Bridge and onto the highway that sped across the borough.

"Welcome to my castle, honey," Harry said forty minutes later, with a wicked grin.

Althea's hand tucked beneath his elbow, Harry leaned on the cane the hospital had given him upon discharge. Behind them, Leonel shifted an armload of groceries as he blinked at the sudden glare. Althea, too, adjusted her eyes.

If the paint cans and rolls of wallpaper neatly piled against the far wall were any indication, they were in a house in the throes of a serious renovation. A very professional-looking toolbox sat beside a five-gallon drum labeled Wallpaper Paste, while trowels and brushes and rags filled a battered, red milk crate. They tiptoed on paint-splattered oak flooring that had seen better days about a hundred years ago.

"I guess they didn't get to the hall yet."

"Maybe we should head over to my place?" Leonel snorted.

Althea drew her coat tightly around her shoulders, trying not to touch anything.

"Don't worry, princess. The paint looks dry to me."

They followed closely as Harry shuffled down the dim hall, ducked through a battered door and flipped on another light.

"As promised," he said proudly, and stood aside to let them pass.

Leonel led with a shake of his head. "I don't know, Harry. Any more surprises?"

Following on his heels, her breath a puff of cold

air, Althea was relieved to step into a room that had thankfully been completed. Freshly painted a pale cream color, with bookshelves overflowing, this was apparently the living room. She watched Harry drop down onto an overstuffed sofa covered with knubby beige Haitian cotton. A thick rug accented the glossy dark-wood floor. A nice room, but no frills or flowers, here. A room designed by a man—that fact a comfort to Althea. End tables, old but newly refinished, held neat stacks of magazines. Cooking magazines, she saw with surprise.

"You cook?" She smiled faintly.

"I try. It was either that or face a future filled with frozen food. Not that I'm ever going to be a threat to Wolfgang Puck. But I was becoming far too well supplied with mac and cheese, boxed or frozen."

"I know what you mean."

The idea of Althea eating macaroni and cheese was too much for Leonel. "Oh, come on, Althea. Living in that big, fancy embassy on l'Avenue Gabriel?"

"I didn't always live on l'Avenue Gabriel, Mr. Murray."

"Perhaps not, but a high-class model like you downing all those cheesy calories? I can hardly believe it."

Althea smiled in spite of herself. "Believe. This is one model who never had to watch her diet. Good metabolism, I guess."

Leonel was disbelieving, but Harry was impatient to show them the rest of the house. "You guys want to save it for dinner? Now you've seen the worst, I want to show you the best."

"This is pretty nice," Althea averred. "My apologies, Harry. The way you described this place, I was worried. But this is really adorable."

"Yeah, I'm actually jealous," Leonel admitted. "I guess you understood what I was talking about, then, when I mentioned wanting to settle down."

"I felt the same way when I saw this place. That's why I bought it," Harry explained, feeling a little bashful as he led them down the draughty hall. He'd never had visitors before. "I hadn't thought about setting down roots, but when the idea came to me about two years ago, well, I guess it was an idea whose time had come. Once I thought about it, it took on a life of its own. When this house came on the market, one thing led to another."

It took some effort, but Harry managed to make it down the dark hall, his cane bearing the weight of his tired body. Marching behind, his friends were nearly blinded by the sudden glare of sunlight that surprised them when he led them through the final door. "Be careful how you step. There might be a nail or two, underfoot."

The kitchen, one day. Right now, though, under construction. Everywhere they looked, lumber was neatly piled. The sheet rock only partially completed, the walls studs were still exposed. New wiring appeared to be in progress, while huge, pink bales of fiberglass insulation took up a complete corner. On the far side, heavy cardboard boxes labeled *Cabinets* stood waiting to be installed. An eight-foot countertop encased in bubble wrap leaned against a wall.

Picking their way carefully, Althea and Leonel circled the kitchen. "Oh, that countertop—is it really granite? Did you pick out the wallpaper by yourself? Oh, my! Leonel, come look at this."

Together, Althea and Leonel peered out a bay window that still brandished the manufacturer's sticker.

"Harry, are we on a pier? Is that actually a boat sitting at the end of a pier? For heaven's sake, old man, you've been holding out on us."

"Harry," Althea gasped, "this is amazing. Are we really in New York City?"

Wobbly on his cane, Harry managed to make it to their sides to share the view. "Yeah, I know what you mean. That's why the interior of the house isn't finished. I asked the carpenters to work on the outside of the house first, while the weather held. Shades of Cape Cod, huh? One look out this window and I wrote the real estate agent a check. The boat was extra, it's just a dinghy, but it was worth every penny. I just wish I were home more to use it. Looks like now I will be."

Leonel was impressed. "Harry, I never would

have guessed. Do you think they have any more homes for sale hereabouts? Maybe I don't have to leave the city to find a decent place to live. But I think," he said, navigating carefully around the kitchen, "maybe you want to call your contractor tomorrow. Unless you want to camp out at my place, Althea? You're more than welcome."

"No need for that," Harry said quickly. "I called them yesterday. They'll be here tomorrow, or the day after at the latest. It might be a little noisy, but they promised to work fast. It's mostly done. A few days and they'll be ready to paint. Actually, Allie, you'd oblige me by helping to pick out some wall colors. You probably have better taste than I do."

"If that living room is anything to go by, you're doing fine."

"She's got you there." Leonel smiled, guessing that Harry was playing any card he could to keep Althea from leaving. "You sure you don't want to rethink this, Althea? You haven't seen the bedrooms, yet. She does have her own bedroom, doesn't she, Harry?"

"Of course she does."

"Well, if you're sure you're staying…" Leonel said.

"I'm staying the night, at least," Althea decided, only the slightest hesitation in her voice.

"Then I guess we had better go bring in the rest of your luggage."

Harry watched them leave, listening to the front

door bang closed. Leaning gingerly on the door-jamb, he looked around with a keen sense of satis-faction. He didn't mind the mess one bit. Hell, he'd lived out of suitcases for so long he wouldn't have minded landing in a pup tent, as long as it was pegged to the ground. He smiled to remember the day the agent had begged him to come out to Brook-lyn, how he had sworn that Brooklyn *really* was a part of the city. It took a weird cab ride through neighborhoods he'd never been to, to get him to Gerritsen Beach. It was a middle-class neighbor-hood, filled with kids riding bikes and playing stick-ball, the day he first saw it. When he saw the house, an ugly, run-down yellow clapboard with utterly no charm, its rotting porch on a precarious angle, he'd nearly laughed himself silly. Only the salty smell of the nearby ocean kept him from climbing back into the cab.

The house had little to recommend it. The front stairs were long gone, it was in desperate need of re-siding, and the windows... Abandoned by its owner, it had stood unoccupied for six years, falling down upon itself as a result. But having come that far, Harry was persuaded to take a look at the interior. He and the agent had piled up some rotting planks to reach the front door, but one step inside the kitchen, one look out this window, and Harry knew he was done house hunting.

Getting a great deal, Harry proceeded to put into

it a great deal—of money! But he knew it would be beautiful one day. His home one day. He hoped Althea could see that. In the meantime, though, he hoped that she didn't mind a little sawdust in her hair and wasn't offended by the pungent smell of paint thinner. Listening to her joke with Leonel as they lugged in her suitcases, he prayed she lasted more than a week—and not because of Leonel's offer— but because of the one *he* wanted to make her.

"Admiring the view?" Leonel asked as he dropped Harry's duffle bag by the door.

Harry's smile was wistful as he gazed out at the docked boats covered with blue tarps and white snow. Waiting for spring. In April he would drive out to Fort Hamilton and sign up for sailing lessons. He would learn how to sail and take care of his boat. April wasn't all that far away, he told himself as he turned to his friend.

"I guess the novelty hasn't worn off," he said with a sheepish smile. "I haven't been here in quite a while, you know, maybe close to a year. I'm pretty tired of traveling, to tell you the truth."

"That's the fever talking. But I can't believe you let me run my mouth off last week about settling down, and here you had this ace in the hole. Why didn't you mention you owned this place?"

"Honestly, I didn't think it mattered. First of all, I was too sick to think straight. And then there was no way I could have persuaded a nurse to stay here with me. But the contractors have been working like mad while I was at Althea's house, and don't think I'm not paying extra for that. I just wish I'd remembered to tell them to leave on the heat," he said, shivering.

"If you tell me what to do with the boiler, I'll do it right now."

Harry waited at the top of the basement staircase until Leonel reappeared. "Done. I heard it kick in. I sure hope it works."

"Oh, it will. It's state-of-the-art, I had it installed first thing, when I bought this place. I wouldn't have brought Althea here if it wasn't. Do you think she would have come, otherwise?"

"But she has."

"Out of necessity," Harry reminded him sadly.

"What are you saying? That the rich and famous Althea Almott is too poor to go to a hotel, if she wished?"

Harry brightened considerably. "I hadn't thought of that."

"Well, do," Leonel advised him with a quirky smile. "And by the way, Harry, I hate to harp on this, but I want to make sure you get that Pulitzer application submitted by February. So try to get some work done. Not get too distracted, if you know what I mean. I was thinking that mudslide stuff was pretty good, definitely worth submitting. The *Times* ran the photos twice, while you were away. On the other hand, *Boston* ran that rainforest sequence for a solid week, and—"

"Leonel, *enough*." Harry sighed, offering his friend a weak apology. "I think I have to lie down, just now, if you don't mind. I think I need to head upstairs."

"No problem, Harry," Leonel said quickly, seeing how pale Harry had become. "It's time for me to leave, in any case."

Even Althea was alarmed when she walked in on them. One look at Harry and she started reading them the riot act.

Amused, Leonel held up his hand. "I'm going, I'm going. I'm running a little late as it is. I have a hot date, and I wouldn't want to keep the lady waiting."

"You?" Harry scoffed as they walked down the hall. "With whom? You haven't had a date in years."

"Well, I have one tonight," Leonel said, slipping into his overcoat. "I'm having dinner with Benicia Ericson."

"Oh, how lucky," said Althea as she joined them. "Where are you going to take her?"

"Anywhere James wants," Leonel said, laughing as he ducked out the door.

"I guess those two are seeing each other," Harry decided as he locked the dead bolt and headed for the stairs.

"Sounds like it, doesn't it?" Althea said thoughtfully as she followed him upstairs. "Benicia didn't mention it last time we spoke, but then, I didn't ask. Oh, what a nice bedroom you have," she said as Harry led the way into the master bedroom.

She watched while he drew back the old-fashioned patchwork quilt that covered his king-size bed. The room was so big it had two large dressers and a rocking chair stationed by a window overlooking the bay. In one corner was a tall bookcase stuffed with books, magazines, a few assorted pieces of pottery and an assortment of family photos. Althea crossed the room to take a closer look.

"Mostly nieces and nephews," Harry explained as he chucked his sneakers across the room and lay down. "Their schools take these pictures every year, and every year my brother and sister send them to me to remind me how much they've grown and guilt me into visiting."

"I forgot that you had a sister and brother. My faulty memory," she apologized. "Shouldn't your family be notified of what is happening?"

Shaking his head, Harry lay down. "I'm much happier being nursed by you than my brother. Besides, I spoke to them when I was in the hospital. My sister, whom I love dearly but who is a royal pain, lives in Sacramento, and my brother lives in Alaska—don't ask—so I told them to stay home. Besides, they both have kids," he added. "It would have been a major hassle for them to be here. And

I'm the one who should apologize. Look at me falling asleep on my first house guest. Please, Althea, sit with me awhile. I can't keep my eyes open much longer, but it would be a comfort to know you're here. Just a few minutes."

"All right, I will. I'll sit right there in that pretty rocking chair, if you hush and promise to go to sleep," Althea agreed. An unnecessary request. Harry's eyes were closing, even as she spoke.

Getting comfortable in the rocker, Althea watched as Harry fell asleep, wondering where it was all going. She didn't fool herself that something was happening, even if she'd declined to discuss it the last time when Harry had pressed the issue. But watching him sleep, something stirred in her.

She *cared* for him, that was it. Her feelings were starting to go beyond the line she had drawn around her heart. Was she being pulled, though, or crossing that line of her own free will? How much of his hospitalization influenced their relationship? Had she been primed to soften toward him every time she visited him at Elmhurst Hospital? Had her pity been aroused unduly? Was it now being transmuted into feelings she might not have, had they met under normal circumstances?

And in the final analysis, did what came *before* matter in light of what she *now* felt? Emotions were a heavy load to bear, she thought, as she rocked back and forth. Hard upon the heels of her divorce, she thought they were also suspect. Too fast, too soon. Something in her was tempted to run, to pick up her bags, open the door and walk out into the snow. She was tempted to dismiss the whole of her heart for the test of time and separation. Part of her must not have faith it would last.

When she was sure he was asleep, Althea tiptoed from the room, making her way down the dimly lit hall to a bedroom Harry had shown her earlier. It was in the part of the house that had been recently painted, its floors newly varnished. Luckily, Harry had managed to furnish it with a bed and an old Shaker-type bureau, along with a battered night table.

Dropping her bag on the dusty bureau, she lit the room's single lamp to bathe the room in a soft, golden glow that made the worn furniture look a bit more attractive. An old corded rag rug provided a little warmth for her cold feet as she walked around the room. After washing, she hung her clothes in a tiny closet and crawled between the cold sheets of the bed. Oh, divine surprise, she thought as she sank beneath a goose down comforter and gloried in the forgiving down of the pillow beneath her head. Thank goodness Harry hadn't stinted on the bedding.

Harry. How nice to drift to sleep on thoughts of Harry. Until, as she lay there in the dark, the cover tucked beneath her chin, she remembered his smothering kiss of days before. Instantly she was awake, her body tingling with the memory of his all-too-sat-isfying touch. She remembered, too, the sexy way his eyes had flashed, concerned that he didn't push her too far, but mad with desire to forge ahead. He had not, for which she was grateful. She hadn't been ready, and somehow he had known. But when there were more kisses, and there would be, she knew that, then what would she do? The passion between them was too intense to be lightly dismissed. Kissing Harry might be an exercise in commitment.

It wasn't the American Embassy, this little house at the edge of nowhere, Althea thought, as she watched Harry putter around the living room the next morning. And if the other houses she had seen upon her arrival were any indication, the neighbor-hood was definitely not wealthy. But there was something here, something special that Harry had been wise enough to recognize and grab hold of for himself. And she had the wit to realize that not so long ago she would have considered the modest house her idea of heaven.

Harry's first day in his home was filled with ex-citement and wonder. Finally he was able to claim it for himself. He must have mentioned a hundred times how thrilled he was to be home, but nothing made up for actually trifling with his possessions, picking out the best spots for his mementos, nesting, as it were.

Settled on the sofa and not wishing to intrude on

his pleasure, Althea watched and was happy for him. His excitement underscored how much he had traveled over the years, how rootless he must have felt, how heavily his feet had landed in this little tract in Brooklyn. It was nice, as well, to simply watch this handsome man and enjoy his rugged beauty, to find pleasure in the grace of his movements. Harry had definitely lost a few pounds and his skin had gone sallow, but there was much in his hard body that he would reclaim, that was already rebounding. Hard-won muscles earned cutting a swath in the brutal jungles of foreign continents still rippled beneath his T-shirt.

The way Harry figured, if he could show interest in his treasures, he must be on the road to recovery. He spent most of the afternoon opening carefully crated boxes. The six enormous boxes Leonel had hauled upstairs for him were only a small part of the huge collection Harry had accumulated during his long decade of travel. Most of the collection was still in storage. Now he had a place to put them. Some of the shipping labels were from out-of-the way places he didn't even remember visiting, until he opened the box to examine the contents. Then he would lift out a piece of artful pottery or an ornate mask, and remember. Or a tiny doll from a village in Zimbabwe that made him smile sadly and made Althea wonder what he was missing. She never asked, for fear of disturbing his privacy. Quietly she would return to her book until he was ready to move on.

Sometimes his intent was to shock her. *Yes, that really was a mummified head. Illegal? I haven't the faintest idea.*

It was one of the most pleasant days Althea had experienced in a long time, and so she told him. He looked at her with such happiness that she felt guilty about never having told him how much she enjoyed spending time with him. Even visiting him in the hospital hadn't been all that much of a chore. The life he had led in the years they had been apart was more interesting than she'd expected.

Beyond his appreciation for her kind words, the look he sent her was eager and tender. "I like you, too, Allie. We could be good together." He didn't add that he had always thought so. He wanted to get beyond reproach.

"As in a new beginning?" Althea asked.

"Why not? I have no objection. Do you?"

Absently she riffled the pages of her book. "I can still count the days that my divorce has been final."

"Yes, but you can also count the months your marriage was over."

Suddenly Harry was beside her, kneeling next to her on the carpet. "It's not like we've just met, you know."

Hypnotized, her entire body on the alert, Althea felt his fingers sketch the contours of her jaw, trace

the tendons of her neck, to slip lower and tug playfully with the button of her shirt. But he made no
other move except to lower his head until their lips
met. His mouth covered hers in a strong hard kiss and
then he was gone. Nestled back among his boxes, he
hummed off-key and acted as if nothing had happened.

Chapter Nine

Benicia and her son, James, arrived with Leonel Murray at around six that evening, hauling two large bags of steaming Chinese food from Leonel's car.

"My saviors," Harry said, grinning as he swung open the door. "I could smell that wonderful food all the way through the door. Come in, come in, it's cold out there. I was wondering how I was going to sustain myself after working so hard all day."

"Overdid it, did you?" Benicia asked as she trundled past with the bags.

"Sleeping is hard work," Harry quipped.

Leonel smiled as he stamped the snow from his boots. "You're looking a helluva lot better than the last time I saw you. I'm glad you're up, because dinner is about to be served, and you have a dinner guest. Master James Ericson, meet your host, Harry Bensen."

James nodded shyly as he followed Leonel into the house, his bashful smile short the usual six teeth of a ten-year-old.

Althea smiled as she stole up behind them and held out her hand. "Hello, James. How do you do? I've been waiting a long time to meet you. Your mother said you were her own personal angel."

Confronted by the sight of what must surely be the most beautiful woman he'd ever seen, James could only stare.

"Yeah, she is kind of pretty, isn't she?" Harry grinned at the little boy. "But she can't cook for beans," he added, trying to set James at ease. "Benicia, did you know that Leonel's mama had seven kids?" he whispered loudly as they moved into the living room.

Benicia was horrified. "Seven?" she repeated, as she helped her son with his coat.

"Harry speaks true. Scary, isn't it, to think of having six brothers," Leonel said with a wink to the little boy. "But that's what we are—seven boys. My mother served spaghetti five nights a week, and my dad ruled us with an iron fist. He had to, every one of us was bigger than him. I'll be wanting a big family, too, once I get going," he said calmly.

"Surely not seven?" Althea gasped.

"Well, maybe not seven," Leonel said with broad smile. "But a few."

"How many is 'a few'?" Harry wanted to know. "Five? Six?"

"A couple is two, a few is three."

"Three kids?" Benicia said with a shake of her head. "I'd be impressed if you found a woman willing to have two."

"Oh, I don't know, I'm checking out the landscape," Leonel said with a wicked grin. "It's not like I wouldn't be able to support a family."

Camping out around the coffee table, they devoured chicken and broccoli provided by Leonel's favorite Chinese restaurant while, amidst a great deal of laughter, they discussed the pros and cons of his future. Althea was the first to lean back, stuffed to the gills, a fortune cookie in her hand.

"Leonel, listen to this. My cookie says, 'Look no more, my lady.'"

"No problem, sweetie, I got the ring right here in my back pocket. So, how many kids do *you* want?"

Althea laughed. "I've never thought about it."

"Oh, come on, Allie, it's a fair question," Harry insisted. "Me, I think I want two, maybe three."

"Not going for a baseball team?" Leonel asked, pushing away his plate.

"You know how much sneakers cost these days?" said Benicia. "You don't want to go there."

Harry scratched his head. "No, I think I'll play it safe. Three kids are plenty. How many for you, Althea? You didn't answer the man."

"Can I start with one and see how that goes?"

Benicia thought that was pretty funny. "See how it goes? If you're expecting a straight path, don't. No such thing when it comes to kids. They pull a ninety in math, they get a forty in English. They get new sneakers, you find a hole in their shirt. You buy them notebooks, they forget to tell you about the lab fees. It's an endless list, and all you can do is negotiate between what they want versus what they need. And that's not always a clear line."

"Isn't that why God invented credit cards?" Leonel suggested.

"Seven kids, huh?" Benicia said, staring hard at him. "I always thought that men ran from that kind of stuff. Family stuff, getting married, kids, that kind of thing."

"Are you speaking from experience?" asked Leonel, his gaze leveled at James, who had fallen asleep on the couch. "I was just wondering if a daddy belonged to this fine young man."

"It wasn't the immaculate conception," Benicia mocked. "Just a clean getaway by a stranger unknown. That's what men do, isn't it—run when things get tough?"

"That's what *you've* learned," Leonel objected. "But if James's daddy wasn't ready for parenthood that doesn't mean you weren't ready for mother-hood. James is living proof, isn't he?"

Her voice cutting, Benicia's vehemence took them all off guard. "Oh, Leonel, you innocent, do you really believe that? I was seventeen when I got pregnant. How *ready* do you think I was?"

"I was referring to the fact that you had the child," he said, somewhat defensive. "That young boy sleep-ing on the couch shows strong evidence that you care an awful lot about him. You're a very brave woman," he added softly.

"Oh, Leonel, I was—am—no braver than a mil-lion other unfortunate girls who ride the trains at night or hide in doorways or sleep on park benches." Benicia looked at James, her brown eyes thoughtful. "He thinks his daddy is dead. I didn't know what else to tell him. I didn't want him to grow up thinking he wasn't wanted."

Althea reached out and covered her hand. "You did the right thing, Benicia. Maybe someday that will all change."

"I've been through the worst. I don't need anyone to get me through the *good* part."

"No, you don't," Althea agreed. "We can see that. But James is such a great kid. Maybe you'll want to share him with someone."

Benicia's look of surprise gave way to a pensive mood as she helped Althea take the dirty plates into the kitchen, but the sight of the half-built kitchen was more than a distraction. "Oh, my God, will you look at this mess?"

"It's not a mess." Althea chuckled. "It's a construction site. At least, that's what I've been told. But it has potential, don't you think?"

"Yeah, *potential*. But does it have running water?"

"A good question. I never thought to ask. The rest of the place does, though. There's a brand-new bathroom upstairs. There was no way I was staying if there wasn't a shower." Althea grinned as they dumped sauce-stained containers into a huge, plastic garbage bag.

"Benicia, you know, back there, when we were talking about children…" Althea took a deep breath. "I've been meaning to say, but I haven't had the nerve."

"What's that?"

"It's more about me than you, actually. When I see you and James together, the way you look at each other, watch each other, your secret little nods…I'm a little jealous. I'm not just saying that. I mean it—I really envy you. It makes me think I would like to have a child, too. Like James, just like James."

"Thank you, Althea. That's very kind of you to say so. I know my good luck, I won't deny it, even if I went about it a little backward. Not that I wouldn't mind a man about the house. It does get a little lonely sometimes, what with it just being me and James. But you know, that's okay, too. I get into the peace and quiet of it, helping James with his homework, snuggling together at bedtime with our favorite books. It's what I'm used to, in any case."

"It sounds wonderful, but have you seen the way Leonel watches you?"

Benicia was suddenly so busy at the sink, Althea wasn't sure if she heard her. "I'm talking about when he thinks no one is looking. And all that talk about kids, like he was issuing a press release."

"You think so? Well, Leonel's a nice guy, just what a girl would like to take home, *if* she were going to take someone home. But I'm not going down any easy road too soon. Been there, done that."

Althea took exception to her assessment. "Leonel does seem nice, but the one thing he does not seem is easy. On the contrary, he's never been married and he must be at least forty, or nearly. That makes him *careful* in my book."

"You want to talk *careful,*" Benicia said, thumping her chest, "here I am, the Queen of Careful. No more mistakes for me, now that I have James to think about. That boy is going to have a good Baptist upbringing, stay off the streets and go to college. Away to college, out of the city, if I have my druthers. Somewhere in New England where the campus square is a lawn of green grass, not a concrete slab. Where there are ten kids in his math seminar, not six hundred. I am bringing James up to *advance,* not to *prance.*"

An Important Message
from the Editors

Dear Reader,

If you'd enjoy reading romance novels with larger print that's easier on your eyes, let us send you *TWO FREE* *HARLEQUIN SUPERROMANCE*® *NOVELS* in our *NEW LARGER-PRINT EDITION*. These books are complete and unabridged, but the type is set about 25% bigger to make it easier to read. Look inside for an actual-size sample.

By the way, you'll also get a surprise gift with your two free books!

Pam Powers

Peel off Seal and
Place Inside...

THE RIGHT WOMAN

she'd thought she was fine. It took Danie words and Brooke's question to make her reali she was far from a full recovery.

She'd made a start with her sister's help and she intended to go forward now. Sarah felt as i she'd been living in a darkened room and some- one had suddenly opened a door, letting in the fresh air and sunshine. She could feel its warmth slowly seeping into the coldest part of her. The feeling was liberating. She realized it was only a small step and she had a long way to go, but she was ready to face life again with Serena and her family behind her.

All too soon, they were saying goodbye and Sarah experienced a moment of sadness for all the years she and Serena had missed. But they had each other now and th t's what

She held

YOURS FREE!
You'll get a great mystery gift with your two free larger-print books!

The Harlequin Reader Service™ — Here's How It Works:

Accepting your 2 free Harlequin Supermance® books and gift places you under no obligation to buy anything. You may keep the books and gift and return the shipping statement marked "cancel." If you do not cancel, about a month later we'll send you 6 additional Harlequin Superromance larger-print books and bill you just $4.94 each in the U.S., or $5.49 each in Canada, plus 25¢ shipping & handling per book and applicable taxes if any.* That's the complete price and — compared to cover prices of $5.75 each in the U.S. and $6.75 each in Canada — it's quite a bargain! You may cancel at any time, but if you choose to continue, every month we'll send you 6 more books, which you may either purchase at the discount price or return to us and cancel your subscription.

*Terms and prices subject to change without notice. Sales tax applicable in N.Y. Canadian residents will be charged applicable provincial taxes and GST.

"And is there no room in this picture for Leonel Murray?"

Benicia sighed. "Althea, I don't know what kind of man Leonel is, and neither do you. We just met. But if you want to have a kid, well, I have to say, I definitely recommend getting a husband first. Hey, wait a minute," she cried, her eyes suddenly wide. "Is that where you and Harry are heading? Althea Almott, do you have anything you want to tell me about Harry? The one lounging around in his jammies, every time I see him?" she added ominously.

"Not tonight."

"Not yet," Benicia countered. "If I remember correctly, you said you met Harry when you first came to New York, when you were a kid. Well, honey, that was a long time ago. Do you always read yesterday's news?"

"Harry is unfinished business," Althea corrected her stoutly. "I just wasn't sure until tonight. There was a moment, tonight…" She shrugged, unable to finish the thought. "I know. I know," she said with a laugh. "The next thing you're going to ask is, What do I do for an encore?"

"*Moi?*" Benicia grinned.

"You say it all the time. And the answer is, I don't know."

"My, oh, my, I do believe I hear a *but* in this conversation. Let me ask you something. If the man was black, would we be having this conversation?"

"Ah, the question of the century," Althea admitted.

"Hmm. And does your mama know?"

"Know what?"

"Know that you're thinking of bringing home a Scandinavian god?"

"I haven't told her anything about Harry."

"From what I remember of your mama, I don't think she's going to be too thrilled. I can just imagine her trotting Harry around the neighborhood to show off to her friends. 'This here's my…my…my…'" Benicia shook her head, a broad smile on her lips. "Sorry, it's hard for me to imagine." She laughed. "Oh, Althea, are you really thinking of dragging baby-blue eyes down to Alabama? Are you really going to take him down to Bobby Jim's Cajun Palace, stuff him with fried catfish and think no one's going to notice that the man is white? Is Harry really going to wheel a shopping cart up and down the aisles of Cleo's Supermarket—oh, I have got to see that one!—and not get himself stared at, till Kingdom come? Speaking of which, ain't he gonna be a *big* hit in church, come Sunday, when the choir starts singing."

"Harry can sing!" Benicia's slow smile told Althea she understood. "Well, aren't we a pair? You with Eric the Red, and me with a Boston Celtic. What *would* they make of us in Birmingham?"

Althea shook her head. "Let's just not plan any weddings any time soon."

Chapter Ten

It was getting on to nine o'clock when Benicia asked Leonel to drive her home. Even if he had banker's hours, she had to be at work early, and James had to go to school. Althea and Benicia watched as Leonel scooped the sleeping child into his arms and carried him to the car. A smile playing on her lips, Althea waved goodbye as they drove away, but Harry seemed preoccupied as he said his good-nights. His silence was a curiosity to Althea, but she was too tired to dwell upon it. When he walked her to her bedroom, she gave him a quick peck on the cheek and closed her door.

When Harry waved a cup of coffee beneath her

nose the next morning, and told her it was nearly noon, Althea was smiling before she even opened her eyes. She heard him raise the Venetian blinds and felt sunshine warm her face. When she blinked, it was to see Harry sitting at the edge of her bed, nursing a cup of coffee.

"Just like in the old days," he teased as he held out the steaming mug. "No makeup, no curlers, only a cup of strong caffeine. And a toasted bagel, if you give me another minute."

"No one uses curlers anymore, silly," Althea said as she reached for the cup. "Haven't you ever heard of blow-dryers and hair irons?"

Harry was incredulous. "Women iron their hair?"

"Harry, where have you been?"

"Nowhere *you've* been, I guess. Can I watch sometime?"

"In about half an hour." Althea smiled as she sipped her coffee. "Right now a shower would do me wonders."

"Yeah, you always did like a hot shower first thing in the morning. I remember a few cozy bubble baths, too." Harry grinned as he played with the strap of her nightgown. On impulse he leaned forward and drew down the satin band. He felt her shudder, though she tried to hide it, when he brushed her bare shoulder with his tongue.

"Althea, I can't stand how we're pretending that something isn't happening between us."

Althea's eyes grew wide at this unexpected turn, and Harry's brow rose in question. "You do know what I'm talking about, don't you, honey?"

"I...um..."

"Come on, Allie, you're not going to sit there and tell me that you aren't feeling *something* for me? I won't believe it if you do."

Uneasy at the insistence in his voice, Althea looked away, but Harry caught her by the chin and pulled her back. She could tell by his look that he was annoyed by her silence, but she didn't know how to respond, and she didn't want to say things she would later regret, just to appease him.

"Look, I'm not asking you to say anything—"

It was amazing how he read her mind.

"And I'm not asking you to *do* anything about it. I just want us to acknowledge that we're working on something here. Is that such a big deal?"

"I suppose not," she said slowly.

"Well, that's big of you," Harry teased, hearing the reluctance in her voice. "I mean, you haven't exactly been fighting me, the few kisses I've stolen from you. As a matter of fact, I think you enjoyed them. Yeah, I thought so," he said, seeing her squirm. "But a man's a man, honey, and, well..."

Didn't she know how lovely she looked, her delicate face a golden flower, her pouty pink mouth begging to be kissed? Didn't she know she left him breathless?

"You look mighty beguiling in that nighty

and…?" Harry struggled for words to explain how he felt, but the more he tried, the sillier he sounded, even to his own ears. Surely to hers, and perhaps he sounded even a bit daunting because Althea had suddenly pulled the covers to her chin, her eyes filled with concern.

Alarmed that he'd frightened her, Harry quickly covered her hand with his own. "Hey, sweetheart, slow down. I would *never* do anything to you… I would *never* force you to do *anything*, Althea, you know that. All I'm saying is you have to confront your feelings, because I think there's something going on here between us that needs explaining."

His words were reassuring, but Althea was relieved when he rose to his feet and straightened the blanket he had creased. The mischievous look he sent her, when he bent to replace her strap, was almost comical. "Well, I'm glad we had this talk," he said, his moth twitching with amusement. "It cleared the air, I can tell."

Althea could barely contain her own smile. "I'm glad you think so."

"I do think so. Only thing better now would be a buttered bagel."

"A blueberry muffin for me!"

"And a mushroom omelette."

"Over light for me!"

"Contrary woman! Can you be ready in twenty minutes?"

"I'm starving." Althea smiled. "I can be ready in ten. And, Harry—"

Harry paused, his hand on the doorknob.

"Thanks for not pushing me," Althea said quietly.

Harry shook his head. "I told you I would never—"

"Harry, meet you outside in ten minutes!"

By the time they were dressed, it was time for lunch, not breakfast. It was Harry's first outing in weeks, and Althea was nervous about whether his strength would hold out, but he promised he knew a restaurant within walking distance. You had to know the exact address to find it, it was so well hidden. It was more like a social club than a restaurant, Harry explained as he tugged on his coat. But the dues were high—the owner had to like you.

Hoping that reporters didn't make a habit of lunching in Brooklyn, they dashed to the restaurant, their hats pulled down low, their scarves covering their lowered faces. Harry held the door open as Althea rushed in laughing, stamping the snow from her boots. Her laughter died as a gray-haired man greeted her with a jaundiced eye.

"Madam?"

"I...um..."

Closing the door behind her, Harry looked over her shoulder. "Aureole," he cried, glad to see his old friend.

"Mr. Bensen! What a pleasure!"

Althea stood aside while the owner greeted his old

customer with an affectionate bear hug. Althea felt as if she had stumbled into the past, something out of a fifties movie, she decided as her eyesight adjusted to the dark barn of a restaurant.

Booths lined either side of the papered walls while a narrow trail of tables ran the center of the room. The seats were covered with red leather while the faded wallpaper was a backdrop for huge posters of Italy. Menus of yellowed parchment were jammed between cruets of olive oil and vinegar, but the red-checked tablecloths that covered the tables were immaculate, and the napkins neatly placed beneath the silverware were starched linen.

A number of customers scattered around the restaurant's tables stood to greet Harry warmly, slap his back and inundate him with questions. Curiously, they said nothing to Althea, but that suited her fine. It was nice to sit back and watch him navigate the room, give everyone his respect and attention, share a few jokes with the elderly men, behaving so kindly.

Watching him, thinking over their time together the past few weeks, she thought she was coming to see the real Harry Bensen. Or rather, perhaps, the man the young Harry had become. Attractive, intelligent, clever, seductive. She saw, too, that Harry was an honest man. The locals would not have tolerated him otherwise.

The meal when Harry finally joined her, would be in honor of Harry's safe return home. So the owner told them as he served up a creamy polenta thirty minutes later. The platters came endlessly. Stuffed mushrooms, baked clams, scungilli fried to perfection, a tender veal scaloppini, cheese-filled eggplant. The works, he said proudly.

Hovering over Harry like a mother hen, Aureole grated his cheese, churned the pepper mill to just the right degree, made sure the bread was perfectly warmed, made sure everything was just right for his favored customer. Nothing was too good for Harry Bensen.

There came a time, though—about when Althea had to grind her own pepper, had to ask Harry to pass her the cheese, and pour her own water—that Althea knew something was going on. That the looks she was earning were too furtive, when it dawned on her that they were as much about the color of her skin as her famous face. They probably didn't know who she was. They only saw that *she was traveling with a white man.*

An accusation hovered in the air, as it often had in the past, vaguely censurious, unspoken, but never quite gone. She looked closer at the faces of the old men toying with their Chianti and was sure she detected more than cursory interest. There was disapproval in their faces, an almost imperceptible downturn of their mouths that had not been there when they greeted Harry. Growing uncomfortable, Althea searched for ways to tell him, but Harry was so pleased with their outing, she hadn't the heart to spoil the meal.

But her friends had done the same thing to him, she recalled. The shock hit her full force. Years ago, in their early years together, when they'd first begun dating. *White bread,* they'd whispered, sensing long before she had that Harry Bensen meant business. With startling clarity, unpleasant memories came rushing back.

Connie Niles had been the most forthcoming. *It won't do your career any good, honey, a fine black woman like yourself getting involved with a white man.* Connie, who had taken the young Althea in hand and laid out the game plan of her future. Landing her protégé on the cover of *Ebony,* within a year. Winning for her, too, the coveted September cover of *Cosmo,* establishing Althea as a force to be reckoned with. Taken under the wing of the magnificent black model Iman, who in turn introduced her to the "holy trinity"—Linda, Christy and Naomi. The fourth musketeer, the press had labeled her.

Told by her friends that black women were only toys to white men—*look at our history, honey*—she declined to become an anecdote. Informed that white men did not actually *marry* black women—*check the statistics, sugar*—she determined not to become another number.

Don't be a fool, Althea. Play with the man all you

like, just don't get caught up in some white man's fairy tale.

But Harry Bensen didn't play games, and, looking back, Althea thought that Harry Bensen might have been the *one* person in her life who hadn't treated her like a product. It was *she* who had not been entirely honest. And she knew now that she had not left Harry *only* because she was preoccupied with her career. In her search for success, she had let go the one good thing she'd had, simply because his skin had been the wrong color. Her biggest mistake—*of course, she could see that, now*—had been to ignore the deafening crash when he slammed the door on his way out.

"Hey, darling," Harry said, reaching across the table to tweak her nose, "a penny for your thoughts."

Startled, Althea jumped. "Sorry. Believe me, you'd be overpaying. You were saying?"

Harry accepted her evasion with good grace. "Leonel and I had a private conversation about careers the other day. Yeah, I knew that would get your attention. Looks like I'm not the only one who might be looking for work."

Surprised, Althea listened quietly as Harry explained.

"It's nothing concrete, Leonel said, just intimations of…mortality."

She heard him laugh but she wasn't fooled. "Aren't your books selling well?"

"Yes, they are, but—"

"And don't they make Torregan a lot of money?"

"Yes, but—"

"And aren't you going to be nominated for a Pulitzer?"

"I guess. I'm not sure."

"Then what is the issue?"

"That's exactly it. I don't know, and neither does Leonel. Like I said, locker-room gossip, a sense of something a little off, but no word, official or otherwise."

"But you have to be worried. You look worried." She frowned.

"Well, I did just get home, and it always creeps me out a little, the first couple of months being in the States. Like supermarkets are off-limits, a bit too much to handle after living in a jungle for six months. Crowds, the subway, that sort of thing, it's an adjustment. Being out of the work loop can make me a bit paranoid, too, which is why I want to hear the specifics from Leonel about what's going on before I drive myself crazy second-guessing my publisher. And then my getting sick threw a real wrench in the works. Yeah, I guess I'm feeling a little shaky, sort of like my life is on hold."

"Poor guy. You're having a terrible time of it, aren't you?"

"Oh, I wouldn't say that, precisely," Harry said, toying with a loose braid that had escaped Althea's hair clip. "But what about you? You having the time of your life? You seemed to be far away a minute ago. You didn't hear me call your name."

Catching one of the older men's wintry looks as Harry touched her, Althea fought a twinge of discomfort. "Harry, have you noticed how everyone's staring at us?"

"Yeah. So? They're jealous." He smiled, stretching his hand across the table to cover hers.

Staring hard at the contrast their skin colors made, Althea smiled sadly. "I don't think so. They are definitely not jealous of your *brown-skinned* girlfriend."

Harry's head spun round sharply to scan the room. He couldn't tell if it was his imagination, but Althea might be right, because suddenly no one was meeting his eyes. No one but Aureole, and his eyes were filled with…what? Uncertainty…reservation…disapproval? *Something* that Harry could hardly believe, but it was gone in the blink of an eye. Althea was right. Suddenly he could feel the many eyes that bored into them as he looked around the room.

"Holy cow… I never…"

"Please, Harry, don't make a scene," Althea begged.

Balling his napkin, he threw it on the table and rose to his feet. "Come on, let's get out of here." Throwing a few dollars on the table, he grabbed Althea's hand and they made their way across the restaurant.

"Harry!" Aureole called as they threw on their coats.

Harry turned slowly, his eyes hard, his voice cold. "Mr. Musante?"

The look the men exchanged said too much, and yet not enough. But Harry's concern was for Althea. He might be looking at Aureole, but his words were for her. "To tell you the truth, I never liked polenta."

His face sagging under the weight of Harry's anger, Aureole understood. They would not be back.

"What do you want to do, apologize for all humanity?" she asked as they marched single file through a pocket path of snow.

"No, just for being an insensitive fool," Harry said, bumping into her when Althea stopped short.

"Forget it, Harry," she said softly as she turned to face him. Shocked to see tears filling his eyes, she cupped his cheek with a gentle hand and brushed his mouth with a light kiss. "My dear Mr. Bensen, you're not a fool, and I'm not dumb enough to hold you accountable for the rest of the world."

"Althea, if I could…but I can't."

"Come on, let's get you home. Some first day out, don't you think?"

Pulling their hats low against the biting wind that had come from nowhere, they walked as fast as Harry's legs would take him, although trudging through the snowdrifts was difficult. Worried that he was susceptible to the cold, Althea was beginning to be sorry they had ever ventured out. Passing a news kiosk, she was annoyed when he stopped. But it was too intriguing. Her face was plastered all over the papers.

Divine Disappearance
    Paris—Althea Almott Boylan, the glamorous wife of Daniel Boylan, the American ambassador to France, has apparently fashioned a timely disappearance just as news of their separation was announced. Confirmation of their divorce was made official by Ambassador Boylan's office at the American Embassy on l'Avenue Gabriel. A well-kept secret, it was announced in *Le Figaro* yesterday morning and hit the newswires immediately. Ambassador Boylan declined to reveal the whereabouts of his ex-wife, except to say that she has returned to the United States. He insisted, though, that the divorce was amicable.

"Yada, yada, yada." Abruptly, Harry hurried past the newsstand, his boots crunching loudly on the snow.
    "Harry!"
    "Have you told him where you are?"
    "Yes, of course I did. Now, will you please slow

down! Daniel is very discreet and would never tell the press where I was. Besides, he can always call my cell phone, if he needs to contact me. We do speak, you know. We were married. Harry, slow down! What on earth are you so angry about?"

"I'm not angry!"

"You could have fooled me," Althea snorted as she hurried after him. "One minute you're—"

And the next minute she was being kissed, hard. A frank message that explained a lot, if only she were listening. She was not. She was past thought, deep in the dizzy expression of passion that enveloped her. Oblivious to the fact that the arms clutching her, the hands holding her upright seemed unusually strong. That the tongue that touched hers chased away all sane thought, that he could have had her there in the snow in the fantasy that flowered. Then, as suddenly she was free, free to cover her mouth with her hand and wonder what had just happened.

"I have a headache," Harry said as he continued down the block, leaving Althea to hurry after him.

Chapter Eleven

Althea was napping the next day when she felt a featherlike touch brush her hip. A soft, almost negligible voice whispered in her ear. "Althea, are you asleep?"

The silly question made her smile. "Yes," she whispered. She gave her hip a little thrust, a question mark. "Can't you tell?"

Ignoring her closed eyes, Harry buried his nose in her hair, its sweet fragrance entrancing. "When I was in the hospital, and I was asleep, I could always tell when you arrived to visit just from the scent of your perfume. What do you call it? I want to remember, for your birthday."

"Angel."

"Angel. A sheer delight—not quite a devil, but you're definitely no angel. Not that I'm in the market for one." Harry's teasing hand roamed. "I like that you respond to me so quickly. I like that I can make you shiver. I like that I can wake you up with my slightest touch."

Althea could feel his lips move along her neck and stretched to give him greater access. Little nips, his soft tongue rimming her ear, made her tingle to her toes.

"Harry…" Slowly, she opened her eyes and turned to face him. He was so charming with his long lashes, his silky yellow hair falling across his forehead, irresistible to touch.

"So blond," she whispered half to herself, reaching up to brush his forehead clear.

"So ready," he said, crawling into bed beside her. Laughing he drew the covers around them both and snuggled into her arms.

"Harry Blue-Eyes," she whispered, as if she had just realized the fact. Her long fingers caressing his cheek, she stared at the contrast of their skin. "I wasn't planning to bring this up, but—"

"But what?"

"It's just that you are…so…white."

"You just noticed?" Harry snorted.

When Althea said nothing, Harry gave up and fell back against the pillows. "We're talking race, here, aren't we? So, what about it? Where are you going with this, since it doesn't matter a tinker's damn to me?"

"It matters to *me,* and it matters to the rest of the world. Remember the way they stared at us at the restaurant?"

"I thought you said you didn't want to talk about that."

"I didn't want to talk about it *then,* but I think we have to talk about it sometime."

"Fine, okay, let's get this discussion over with. So, the world has noticed that you're black, I'm white and we're together. What of it? People stare at everything. Talk about getting eyeballed, try photographing a mountain village in Nepal. I guess I've become a little thick-skinned, no pun intended. Hasn't your own traveling inured you to the stares of others?"

"I guess we don't travel in the same circles."

"Maybe it's the woman in you."

"Maybe it's the African in me."

Harry could barely hide his irritation. "Althea, why don't you come out and say what you really mean? If you're worried about something, just say so. I really don't want to have my sex life politicized."

"You…me…" She hesitated.

"I've been to this movie before, haven't I?" Harry growled as he swung his legs over the side of the bed and cradled his head. "If I'm in the middle of a rerun, Althea, please, tell me now, because if I am, I have no intention of sitting through the rest of this film."

Glaring, Althea scrambled to her knees. "If you feel like you are in the middle of a rerun, it may be because you never stayed to see the end of the movie!"

"Well, hell, I wanted to! *You* were the one who kicked me out of your life, Althea. *You* were the one who asked me to leave."

"And you didn't make any bones about packing your bags, either. *You* were gone so fast, I didn't have time to…to…"

"To *what*, Althea?" Harry shouted, his anger at full throttle. "Did you even know what you wanted?"

"Get your story straight, Harry," she hissed. "I was barely voting age. I'm sorry if you were hurt, but we were both very young. Surely you can forgive me for that."

Harry sat beside her, impatiently running his hand through his hair. The misery of the past was still fresh in his mind, but she seemed unable to give him credit for having been hurt. In all their discussions, it had always seemed to him that it was *her* story.

"Look, I'm sorry for getting so upset. It's just that— It was about race then, too, Allie. Don't think I didn't know it. All right, I'll let go of that baggage, it's long overdue. But we can't say we're young anymore. It wouldn't be much of an excuse. If this is about race, if this is about the color of our skin, if you don't want this—*us*—to go any further, I'll understand, and no hard feelings. No question, this is tough stuff. But I really, really hated leaving you ten years ago, and I don't want to go through that agony twice. Tell me the truth while there's still time for me to bail out."

Althea stared at Harry, unsure what to say. "Harry, I don't have any answers. How can I know what the right thing is to do? I don't want to hurt you, but how can I promise not to?"

"Then just answer me this, Althea. Are you putting yourself on the line? Because, dammit all, *I know I am.*"

She met his accusation with determination in her eyes. "I *think* I am."

Harry sighed with relief. "Well, that's something, I guess. If I at least know that you're willing to give us a chance, I think I—*we*—can deal with everything else. At least, I hope we can."

"But, Harry, it really is hard for me to face down stares from other people. That incident wasn't the first time that's happened to me. Being married to an ambassador put me in a place where those things didn't happen, where I was protected from that sort of treatment. I had forgotten…"

Althea took a deep breath and started over. "I had forgotten what it meant to be black, in an uppity, white-bread restaurant."

Harry wound his arms about her and drew her close. "Althea, if I could only change things. I told you then and I'll say it again, but I can't. If I only could. I don't know what else to tell you, Allie. The world isn't going to change for us—no time in the near future, that I can see. Does that mean we should miss out on the good thing between us? We'll just have to pick a better class of restaurants," he teased.

Althea's ambivalence was written across her face, but the doorbell sent the couple scrambling from the bedroom with just enough time to dress. It was the carpenter crew, come to work on the kitchen. Quickly, they bagged a few books and left in search of the tea lounge they'd noticed the day before, where they would be allowed to linger over their coffee. They passed two hours there, until Althea grew restless and announced that, the snow notwithstanding, she needed some air. Beginning to regain his strength, Harry was in total agreement. It was a glorious sunny day. The wind was down and it was fifty degrees. How could they resist?

Bundling up, they tossed their books back into their backpacks and wandered down the avenue. Fifty degrees was an unheard-of treat for a winter's day in New York. They were able to window-shop with ease. Althea considered it good therapy for Harry's weakened body.

"Oh, Althea, you would think shopping was good therapy for a cold sore," Harry said, laughing.

Searching out the oddest things to buy, they were soon filling their backpacks.

"Look at all this fruit," Althea said, as a display

of bright-red mangoes caught their eye. "I haven't shopped like this in years. Peaches from Chile, pineapple from Hawaii, oranges from Israel, Chinese apples from— You don't really think they're from China, do you?"

Harry threw an arm around Althea's shoulder and drew her close. "I think," he said, whispering in her ear, "that those Chinese apples—pomegranates, if you prefer—are from…the supermarket down the street." Laughing loudly, he pulled Althea close and kissed her hard on the lips. Althea was mortified. Peeking past his shoulder, she wriggled from his grasp when she saw a passerby grinning broadly.

"Hey, everybody, this *is* my girl," Harry shouted gleefully as complete strangers rushed by. It wasn't much of a kiss because Althea was laughing too hard, but he tried to kiss her again.

"Oh, Harry, get away from me." She laughed as she swiped at her mouth. "That kiss was sloppy and wet and…embarrassing."

"Oh, you want more, do you?" Grinning wickedly, Harry swung Althea into his arms and bestowed another euphoric kiss on her laughing mouth.

"Now, where were we?" he said as he set her back down on her feet. "Oh, yes, mangoes, yeah, we definitely need some mangoes."

"You need to calm down," Althea retorted.

"I can't," Harry protested happily. "The sun is

out, I've got my girl by my side, and I'm alive. How can I not be excited?"

"Harry." But when Harry would not be restrained, Althea dashed into the fruit store with an armload of mangoes and apples. "I'll just get these weighed."

"Sure, honey. I'll wait outside."

"Nothing like you're used to, is it?" Harry observed when Althea reappeared, minutes later. He motioned to the window of the jewelry store where he had parked himself, the rows of silver and gold trinkets winking up at them, colorful semiprecious stones sparkling in their velvet beds.

"A girl wouldn't turn down a diamond from *anywhere*," Althea said matter-of-factly.

"Is that so?"

"That's so."

"Then wait here and don't move," Harry ordered her, and before she knew it, he was making funny faces at her from the other side of the jewelry store window. She watched as he cornered the jeweler and pointed to a topaz ring.

"Harry, no!" she mouthed. Awkwardly, she tried to gather their clumsy bags and follow him inside, but Harry was back on the sidewalk, standing beside her before she could stop him.

"Thus speaketh spontaneity." He bowed as he handed her a black velvet box, a look of satisfaction on his face.

Althea dropped the bags she was clutching and

lifted the tiny lid. Just as she feared, an exquisite topaz ring winked back at her. "Harry, it's lovely, but you shouldn't have. Didn't you see me motion to you?"

But Harry ignored her. "He said it could be sized. It's a six-and-a-half. I guessed."

"You guessed right." Althea smiled. "But I can't wear it. It suggests something far too…serious."

"Hey, didn't you just say that a girl would never turn down a diamond?"

"You, Mr. Bensen, are playing word games with me. I was speaking hypothetically."

"What's the difference?"

"The difference is the state of our relationship. The degree of a commitment is reflected in a gift. I'm not ready for this."

Harry's face fell. "You'll share my bed but you won't wear my ring? I don't understand."

"I share your bed because I like you very much, but taking jewelry from you would change the equation. It would color it in a way that would make me uncomfortable. I don't want this sort of gift from you."

"Can it be a thank-you for nursing me back to health?"

"Harry, please don't make this issue bigger than it should be. If you want to thank me, fine. A box of Swiss chocolates would be great. A topaz ring is too serious."

"Come on, Allie, this isn't Tiffany's, for Pete's sake, and that isn't the Hope Diamond." Harry was mocking, but Althea could see that his feelings were hurt.

"It's too serious," she insisted softly.

"It's not an engagement ring, if that's what's worrying you. It's a friendship ring. We're friends, aren't we?" he asked, his brow furrowed in question.

"I don't need a ring to remind me of that."

He might feel romantic, but the art of persuasion was unknown to Harry Bensen. Irritation and a short temper were more his style. When he threw up his hands, his disgust was evident. And his disappointment undeniable. "Okay, okay. How about a compromise? You wear it on a chain around your neck, and I won't say a word. For friendship's sake. Oh, come, Althea, don't *you* make such a big deal," he sighed. "Believe me, honey, it wasn't all that expensive. Hell, I couldn't begin to buy you anything remotely like what you've probably got hidden away in your vault. But I enjoyed buying you *something,* and I only want to see you wear it because *I* gave it to you."

Althea shook her head and replaced the ring in its box. "How about if I think about it?" Although she knew he wasn't asking her to marry him, a ring was special. Fresh from a divorce, landing on her wobbly feet back in the States, Althea was bent on rethinking her life as much as her career. Her plate was full, and now here was Harry pressuring her to take their relationship to the next level.

Perhaps she shouldn't have shared his bed. Perhaps she ought to think about slowing the pace, especially in light of his gift. But judging from the look on his downcast face, he wasn't in agreement. Neither said much as they trudged home.

Chapter Twelve

Althea kept the topaz ring but decided to return to her own apartment. Harry's gift had made things too complicated. It set off a host of feelings she wasn't ready to confront. Too bad he hadn't given her a box of handkerchiefs. She wouldn't have been nearly so concerned.

Her ex-husband calling that night on her cell phone was the icing on the cake. Daniel was not pleased to hear that she was—in his words—shacking up with another guy. In the icy, clipped voice he saved for reporters, he informed her that such behavior was "unbecoming" the wife—

Ex-wife, Althea had reminded him.

Fine. *Ex*-wife of an ambassador. Especially in light of the fact that the ink on their divorce papers wasn't even dry. She was to take herself home, at once, or he would—Daniel would never be so crass as to threaten her, but his words hung fire—not be happy.

Deep down, though, she thought Daniel had a point. It was somewhat in line with the point she had been trying to make to Harry. Too much, too fast. But to tell Harry about Daniel's phone call was to invite disaster, so she opted out of that line of defense. Harry ranted and raved, but two days later she packed her things, and when he came downstairs, she had already called a cab. When he saw her bags by the door, his eyes grew dark.

"You're running away again, Allie, that's what you're doing."

"From what? Not from you," she said, peering out the window for her taxi, hoping it would arrive before this escalated into another full-blown argument. The one they'd had the night before had been a beaut, and she was emotionally drained.

But Harry wasn't buying it. "Yes, you are, you're running from me and all because of a lousy dime-store ring. I knew the minute I saw your face that I shouldn't have bought it."

"I'm wearing it around my neck, aren't I? See?"

But Harry wasn't interested in being placated. "You're wearing it to keep me quiet, so you can sneak out of here without feeling guilty. God, I hate being made a fool of twice in one lifetime."

"Twice?" Althea laughed uneasily. "Harry, are you trying to make me feel guilty?"

"You're leaving, aren't you?" he snapped, his voice thick with accusation. "And don't think I'm going to shoulder the blame for our breakup. This one's on you."

"Harry, I am not breaking up with you. Breaking up? You make it sound like we're seventeen, for goodness' sake. I adore you, but I need some space. I've only been back in the States a couple of months. There were things I was intending to do, and you weren't one of them. I don't mind having been sidetracked by you. On the contrary, I like having you back in my life. I just don't want you to *be* my life."

"If I recall correctly, you said the same thing the last time you walked out on me."

"I did not walk out on you. Well, not precisely." Althea flushed. "You could have hung around a bit longer, fought for your rights. But you didn't, did you?" she snapped, her turn to be judge and jury. "Instead you vanished into thin air. Your note was longer than your lease."

"And where is yours?" Harry said, furious at her accusation.

"You're right. I didn't write you a note, but I didn't sign a lease this time around."

Drawing a hand over his worn, pale face, Harry rubbed his eyes. "Allie, don't do this," he said quietly.

"I have to, Harry." Lord, how she hated to hear the

unhappiness in his voice. But perhaps there *was* something he could understand. "All right, you want to know the truth? Connie Niles called."

"That witch."

"That witch wanted to know if I would come back to work. Finally, she's been getting calls asking about me. She even lined me up with a job for February Fashion Week, the one here in New York, so I won't have to travel. Don't you see, we won't have to be apart? But I have to go home. There are things I need to do to get ready."

"How come you didn't mention this before?"

"I'm mentioning it now."

"All right, great, fine. But why is our being together and your going back to work mutually exclusive?"

"Because it is."

"Why?"

"Why, why, why," Althea sighed. "Well, partly because you hate Connie Niles."

"I do not hate Connie Niles. I just don't like her, is all."

"Be honest, Harry. Quite frankly, I think you hate the entire modeling industry, and that's not going to help me in the long run. It's…it's unsupportive. And…and besides, you're a distraction," Althea added, near the end of her rope. "I know you're on the mend now, but you're so…needy. Sometimes I can't think straight, and right now I need to concentrate."

"You've made yourself the number one priority of your whole life."

"Oh, that's so unfair given I've been nursing you for weeks."

"Okay, okay, maybe it is a little, but it just goes to prove. I mean, what about all the good things between us, the fun, the talks, the way we've been getting on? Doesn't that count for something?"

"Of course it counts, but listen to yourself. You're suffocating me."

Interrupted by the blast of a car horn, Althea was relieved. The cab had pulled up just in time. The lump in her throat was threatening to strangle her. Ignoring Harry's sad look, she grabbed her bags and gave him a quick kiss. "Harry, you'll be fine. I'll call you first thing in the morning." He didn't answer, his face spoke more eloquently than words.

Watching her stow her bags in the trunk, climb into the cab and drive away, Harry stood by the window for a long time afterward, lost in thought. The gray pall of the overcast sky weighed heavily on his shoulders. His whole mood was a rainy day. Why, he wondered, were things always so complicated between them? They had been so happy the past month. Why did she seem to fight her happiness?

Suffocating her, she had said. Indeed. How melodramatic. The woman should be a bloody actress. It was playing just like the first time they broke up. He remembered very clearly how she had come home one afternoon and told him it was over. Just like that. It was raining that day, too, he remembered, when she asked him—no, told him—to pack his things and leave. And just like today, she had refused to give him a good reason. Self-righteous and uncompromising, she had been a stranger. He couldn't leave fast enough for her.

Now they were strangers again. Oh, he knew what she *said,* but he was unsure what she *thought.* Was it a matter of once burned, twice shy? Did it matter? Because if she thought he was going to give up on them as quickly this time around, she had another think coming.

Althea arrived home late that afternoon and fell right into bed. She didn't even bother to unpack her belongings, she was so tired, especially after that final scene with Harry. When she awoke later, she had just enough energy to order some take-out from the local Thai restaurant. She almost never watched television, but it definitely seemed in order tonight. She stayed up until three in the morning, watching reruns.

The next morning, she made herself a cup of coffee and carried it into the little office she had set up in the extra bedroom, adjacent to the living room. It was gratifying to see that her office phone machine was blinking. The last few times she was home, her machine had been so quiet, she thought she had fallen from earth. It had been the same with her cell phone. But now that the red light was flashing, maybe word had gotten round that she was back in New York. Maybe those obnoxious reporters who hounded her were good for something.

The first call she returned was to her agent, Connie Niles. "The runway job is still on, not to worry, sweetie. I just wanted to be sure you got my message about the grapevine. They're saying that if it weren't for me, you wouldn't have a job. I wanted to warn you. Didn't want you to be caught off guard."

"How dare they!" Althea spluttered, she was so angry. "Who started that rumor, do you know?"

"If I had to hazard a guess," Connie said bluntly, "I think she might have long blond hair and be Czechoslovakia's most valuable export. Next to beer, of course," Connie quipped.

"Isabella Goth."

"No names, please. I have no proof. Come, come, Althea, you're no babe in the woods. No one's going to make it easy for you. You're a brand name, and these young chickies are easily threatened. Or have you forgotten how it was?"

That was not much consolation, Althea told Connie before she hung up, but she supposed that forewarned was forearmed. In a snit, she went back to sifting through her mail, but it was a chore of

lazy intention. She really didn't want to do anything in particular on her first day back home, but
with February Fashion Week fast approaching, she
ought to be sure her invitations were in place. If
they'd been forwarded to Paris, it would be a major
problem.

Sorting them from the bills was a major pain, but
she was relieved to see that all the big names were
there. Calvin Klein, Donna Karan, Kenneth Cole,
Marc Jacobs. And the party invites, too, an assortment to warm her heart. The Alice Roi party might
turn out to be a bit grungy, but she wouldn't say no
to the Louis Vuitton bash. They could always be
counted on to throw a spectacular affair. And no matter what, she was *not* going to miss the Victoria's
Secret Valentine's Day celebration. They always had
the best deejay. Harry might not dance—he hadn't,
way back when, although things did change—but
she thought it wouldn't be too hard to get him to escort her to that particular affair.

Speaking of which… Dropping everything, she
picked up the phone and dialed his number. "Hello,
Harry."

Harry's greeting was curt. "Althea."

Making a face at the phone, she proceeded to ask
him how his day was.

"Allie, I just woke up. It's only eight-thirty."

"Oh, yeah, right."

Silence.

"Um, well, I was just having some coffee and wanted to say hello. Have any special plans for today?"

"Yeah, I was thinking of a shower. Maybe brushing my teeth. But I don't like to rush things."

Oh, yeah? Great. Moving right along. "Seriously, how are you feeling this morning?"

"Fine, thanks. I'm walking."

"Oh, good, fine." She refused to let him get her upset. "I'm fine, too, since you happened to ask."

"Glad to hear it."

"Well, the reason I called, I mean *one* of the reasons I called, not the main reason, of course, but—"

"Althea."

"Harry, you could make this call a little easier for me."

Harry was appalled. "You want me to be nice? After the way you've jerked me around?"

"It's an idea."

"You might say I'm a little angry at you so being nice is not going to happen right this minute. Give me a week."

"Harry, you are being *so* unfair."

"Allie, did you call to argue or did you have something you wanted to ask me?"

Althea wasn't sure she wanted to ask him anything anymore, the way he was sounding. "I need an escort to a party."

His sneer was close to graphic. "Oh, right, a party. Just what the doctor ordered."

"I thought you would appreciate the diversion," she said, on the defensive.

"A good choice of words. What did you have in mind?"

"It's formal, you'd need tails—"

"As in tuxedo or the devil?"

"Maybe we'd better stick to a jacket. You're not the formal type."

"What's the occasion?"

"The Victoria's Secret party." Althea could almost see him smile over the phone.

"Now, *that's* a party I will gladly attend. I don't boogie, but I do a mighty fine drool."

Althea grimaced. "That's what I thought. I'll bring lots of tissues. But it's not for a week, so how about dinner tomorrow? Or Thursday, if you prefer?"

Their plans solidified, Althea hung up, collapsing in her chair at the effort it took to make the call. Perhaps she shouldn't have called him so soon. She supposed that, from his point of view, he had a right to be mad. On the other hand she wanted him to know that she was sincere about keeping their relationship going, and she wasn't going to allow his bad temper to dictate her behavior. If she wanted to call him, she would. If he wanted to hang up… But he hadn't.

Opening the top drawer to her desk, a pretty oak escritoire she had picked up for a song at the Twenty-

Sixth Street Flea Market, she searched for her address book. If the Red Door Salon could fit her in that afternoon, she would take the spa's first available appointment, her nerves were that frayed.

Of course they could. "For Madame Ambassador, always. Welcome back, Madame Ambassador. Two o'clock, then, Madame Ambassador."

Althea wondered how much mileage they were going to wring from that title. Way past her divorce, she was sure. Never mind, she told herself. If it got her an appointment, they could call her whatever they wished. Making her way up Fifth Avenue, it crossed her mind to send the bill to Harry because it was really all his fault that she was so stressed out. But after a Swedish massage, a seaweed body wrap and an hour in the nail salon, she felt so much calmer she gladly paid the bill.

Alone again that evening, she ordered in soup and a grilled turkey salad from a local Greek diner. Adding a glass of cold Chablis to the menu, she snuggled into bed, a tray carefully perched across her lap. Only the presence of Harry sitting beside her could have made her happier. Looking around her cozy bedroom, Althea had to smile. People thought models led such spectacular lives, and sometimes they did, but by and large she knew that *she* was happiest with a hot meal and a good book. Having bought three romance novels on the way home from the spa that afternoon, she was in heaven.

Early the next morning she joined a gym and met with their personal trainer to work out an exercise program. An hour later she was on her way to Vidal Sassoon's, where she was scheduled for a haircut and highlights. Having set up a lunch date with Benicia over on Columbus Circle, she hurried across town the moment her hair was done.

Already seated, Benicia greeted Althea with an infectious grin. "Wow, girl, don't you look terrific."

Out of breath, Althea returned her hug and collapsed in a chair. "Hi, Benicia, and thanks. You don't look too bad yourself."

"Been running around like a maniac?" Benicia chuckled as Althea caught her breath. "My goodness, will you look at all those curls. I didn't know you had so much hair. Those gold highlights are stunning, just the right touch. Perfect."

"Are you sure? You're telling me the truth, aren't you? My regular colorist was on vacation so I had to try someone new."

"I think I'm going to get my hair done the same way, if it's all right with you. Would that be proof enough?"

"That would do nicely, and it would be very becoming."

"So what have you been doing besides your hair?"

"I've been working hard all week to pull myself together. I just joined a gym this morning. I hadn't worked out once since I left Paris. You should have seen me sitting in the hot tub afterward, just so I could walk. My legs were killing me when I got off the treadmill."

"Hey, your body is your temple. You have to do what you have to do. How have you been otherwise?"

A waiter swung by to hand them their menus, but Althea was too excited to order, so Benicia ordered for them both. "Two Cobb salads, please. Is that all right, Althea? I'm starving." Althea nodded, and the waiter left to fill their order.

"This may sound silly," Althea confided, as she helped herself to a roll from the bread basket, "but a year away from the catwalk is a long time in my profession. Six months can be a lifetime. And what with my marriage and going to live in Europe, it's going to be close to about two years since I've worked."

Benicia clucked sympathetically. "Althea, from what I've heard, you've paid your dues. You're as high profile as any woman can be. You're beautiful, rich and famous, and you have clout. No one can fool with that, so what are you worried about?"

"I'm not exactly Oprah," Althea said thoughtfully as she buttered her roll.

But Benicia was right. The life Althea had led on the runway had been a good teacher, and she had been lucky in many respects. She'd had an impressive career and worldwide recognition, had made a fabulous marriage, even if it hadn't lasted. Too, she had been able to care for her mother, had been able to put away a substantial amount for both their old ages. If the climb had been less agreeable than she'd hoped, if some of her sacrifices were greater than she'd expected—her thoughts lit on Harry—well, it was a very competitive business. No one lacking in backbone should try it. Her ambitions had been met and would be again. It was only that this time round she would try to be more sensible. She would try to surrender less of herself, make fewer personal sacrifices. Like Harry.

But these things she could not share. It was better to point her thoughts in other directions, equally worrisome, but less private.

"I think that part of me is afraid of being perceived as…old."

"Old?" Benicia gasped. "At twenty-eight? Wow. I guess…maybe. But, wait a minute. Look at Lauren Hutton, churning out that new line of makeup. Nobody stays in modeling forever, Althea, and there are so many other options these days. Public relations, magazines. Even Tyra Banks has branched out, starting that girls' camp. There *is* life beyond what you know. You have to do your homework, is all."

"How do you know all this?" Althea asked doubtfully.

Benicia's brown eyes held a mischievous gleam. "I go to the dentist a lot. Hey, I know a home for unwed mothers that could use a good spokesperson."

"You mean yours?"

"Sure I mean mine," Benicia said with a laugh. "I'm not above waving my own flag. But there's a whole slew of worthy causes that would gobble you up. Like I said, you have the power. Maybe you want to think about doing something with it."

Althea studied her plate, nibbling absently at her salad, a faraway look in her eyes. She felt as if she was seeing her future for the first time. "Maybe I will," she said slowly.

"You should. You did the modeling gig. You did the husband trip, Madame Ambassador. Now is a good time to do the Althea thing."

Althea's thoughts flashed back to Harry. Now might be a good time to do the Harry thing. It would take some figuring, but she did not want to leave him out of the picture.

Benicia almost seemed to read her thoughts. "You know, Althea, I've tried calling you a number of times, and when I couldn't find you, I called Harry, but he blew me off."

"Harry," Althea groaned, falling to earth with a thud.

"Uh-oh. That doesn't sound good. Come to think of it, he wasn't too friendly."

"Harry Bensen is boiling mad because I moved back to my apartment. When I told him I needed some breathing space, he got all crazy. I can still hear him yelling. Last time I saw him, he was steaming."

"And of course you yelled back."

Althea shrugged matter-of-factly. "I couldn't help it. He was so impossible, so insistent."

Benicia gave her friend a sweet musing look. "Sounds like Harry wants you to move back in."

Althea's laugh was two shades sardonic. "If I asked, I think he would pack my bags for me."

Fingering the tiny ring that dangled from her necklace, she knew that whatever she wanted from Harry was a barely conscious thought, nothing she dared to put into words just yet. She knew that he lingered somewhere in her future, even if she had only begun to touch upon her secret dreams, but she was still reeling from the shock of her divorce. He knew that, and knowing that, she thought he should try to be more patient.

The truth was, no matter what anyone thought, she had *never* expected Daniel to ask for a divorce. But that was not something she was ready to share—maybe not ever. She had committed to him because he was interesting, handsome and powerful. A good man, too. A fine man, and honorable—a heady combination for a country girl from the South. Unfortunately, now that it was over and they had some distance, she could see that love had never been part of the equation. She had mistaken Daniel's affection for passion, his instinct to comfort for genuine need.

More fool her. It had only been a marriage of convenience. When she had finally confronted him, it had been painful to hear his devastating assessment of their marriage.

"Didn't you have everything you wanted?"

"I wanted *you,*" she had cried.

"It was never part of the bargain," he'd said gently. "Don't you remember? We were going to be the quintessential black couple, Mr. and Mrs. Fame and Fortune. Loving was never part of the deal."

"But I thought… I had hoped…"

"You shouldn't have."

Stirring her tea, Althea sat lost in thought until Benicia waved her hand. "Hello in there. Earth to Althea."

Although her unhappiness was hard to miss, Althea managed a lopsided smile. "Sorry."

Benicia brushed it off with a short laugh. "I won't pry. I know you have a lot going on, Althea, but try to think of it this way. You're just going through a little period of adjustment. And, boy, am I hating to be the one to tell you—my feelings about men in general not running that high—but Harry Bensen is a good man. He really is. He's so crazy about you, it's almost embarrassing. Still, no matter what he says, you don't have to make any decisions anytime soon, so why not just enjoy the party? The way that virus caught up with him—he *has* been pretty sick— maybe he's just not operating on all four cylinders. Would it be so bad if you cut him some slack?"

"I suppose not. I do adore the big buffoon. I have to admit, though—just between the two of us, mind you—when my agent called the other day, there was something…a part of me was so relieved that I practically ran out the door. I'd been floundering, unsure what direction to head, and *so* not sure what was even available that any job offer would have been a godsend. The job my agent got me is going to be a terrific boon. It will feel good to be heading back in front of the lights in a few days. Maybe I didn't land any long-term contract, but it's good work, nonetheless."

"Do you usually work under a contract?"

"I'm black, Benicia. I don't *ever* expect a contract, not long-term, in any case. You know Liya Kebede, that gorgeous black model from Ethiopia? You've seen her around, you just don't know her name. Liya just signed a multimillion-dollar contract with Estee Lauder. They've been selling makeup for over fifty years and they never had a black model under contract until last April."

"Well, but they do now."

"Yes, they do. And it's not like *no one* hires black models, although I have to say, they are fewer and fewer, these days. Not that it was anything to get excited about ten years ago, when I first started. I was living under a lucky star in those days, to get any work. Most of my success was due to my agent going to bat for me. Oh, sure, you see the big names and their gorgeous faces, but by and large, the faces of color are few and far between in the pages of haute couture rags. So, getting this job is a big coup. Only, Harry doesn't think so," Althea sighed.

"Did he say so?"

"Not precisely. But he didn't seem to appreciate the part where I said I had to focus. Running around the past few days, the way I have, he would have hated it, he would have said I was being frivolous. He doesn't understand the industry, and he never did, to tell you the truth."

"Well, he *is* sort of an earth child, so I can see how he wouldn't get too excited about body sculpting and spin classes and makeup and stuff. But I was under the impression he was ready to give it a try."

"Harry wants to pick up where we left off a hundred years ago. He wants a home and kids. You heard that for yourself. I'm not sure I'm ready to give up my waistline," Althea said with a sour grin.

"This girl just wants to have fun?"

"No. This girl wants to pick up the pieces of a career she should never have dropped. I gave up Harry to make a better life for myself, and it hurt, let me tell you. Then I traded my self-sufficiency for the agenda of my husband. I did it willingly, I won't say otherwise, but there always seemed to be a choice to make. Career versus happiness. Some things never change, do they? But why must I choose? In some respects being with Harry is the same as being with my ex-husband. And then there are all the things Harry takes for granted, and I know it's because he's white. That's an issue, too."

Her chin resting on the heel of her hand, Benicia was mesmerized. "Like how, for instance?"

"Well, how about this? The way Harry struts around this old globe, for instance, taking his funny pictures, taking for granted he can go anywhere and be welcome. Well, I can't do that. We had lunch one afternoon in a restaurant where I was so incredibly uncomfortable, so unwelcome, all because I was black. Harry *never* has to think about that. He didn't even notice until I mentioned it."

"What did he do when you told him?"

"We left, of course."

"Well, that's something."

"Oh, he's not obtuse, I'll give him that. He's well traveled and extremely educated. It's just that he takes it for granted that if we really wanted to, we could make a go of things. He doesn't see the same obstacles I do, and I'm beginning to wonder if it's a race thing, on his part. Unconscious maybe, but there. All that blond hair getting in his eyes obscuring his vision, maybe. He gets really annoyed when I bring up the subject, but he's white, what does he know? I mean, he knows *stuff*, but he doesn't know about being black, does he? He gets mad, accuses me of playing the race card. Like I have any other card to play," Althea said with a sad smile. "Hey, is this making any sense?"

"Yes," Benicia said, with a tiny shake of her head. "He's not black, is what you're saying. Okay then— and don't yell, but I have to ask—do you think maybe *you're* putting too much emphasis on race?"

Althea nodded. "I've thought about that."

"Do you love him, Althea?" Benicia asked quietly.

"The problem is, yes, I think so," Althea admitted.

"Then I guess you do have a problem, sweetie."

"What problem? The doctor is in."

Althea and Benicia looked up to see Leonel Murray looming over them, a big grin on his dark face. He pulled out a chair, giving Benicia a quick kiss before he sat down. "Hello, ladies."

"Oh, I hope you don't mind, I forgot to say." Benicia gave Althea a quick apologetic glance. "I asked Leonel to join us."

"Excuse me, have I been on the moon?" Althea said, her brow high. "Because I think I've missed something."

Leonel smiled as he laid a huge portfolio on the table. "Don't get too excited, Althea. We're just trying each other on for size. But it seems like a good fit so far, doesn't it, Benicia?"

Benicia smiled, but didn't answer Leonel's question directly. "James seems to like him."

They paused to watch their waitress hurry over, pour Leonel a cup of coffee and take his order. "We were just talking about Harry Bensen," Benicia continued, as their waitress left. "From what Althea says, it sounds like he's bored."

"Well, ladies, he won't be bored much longer," Leonel said, putting the portfolio he had just laid down. "I'm on my way over there as soon as I finish eating, to deliver the final proof of his book. This bundle will keep him busy, I promise you, that and getting him to fill out the Pulitzer prize application."

"Do you really think he has a chance?" Althea asked, spearing a forkful of lettuce.

"I wouldn't encourage him otherwise. Don't get me wrong, that man's health is still a major issue, and if he doesn't take care, he could suffer a relapse. He may be getting better, he told me he's been getting out for brief walks, but his illness has taken its toll. If I know Harry—and I *do* know Harry—he's overdoing things. Some old-fashioned paperwork will slow him down. And did he mention to either of you the bad news I gave him the other day? I hated to be the messenger," Leonel said in a rush, as he cleared his throat, "but Torregan Publishing decided to put a hold on his next trip. He was none too happy to hear that, as you may imagine."

"That explains his happy mood," Althea sniffed.

"Could be. When Torregan heard he was in the hospital again, they put their foot down. Collective feet, I should say. This goes all the way to the top. They have no quarrel with his work. On the contrary, they have no idea how they are going to fill the gap. They just don't want to be responsible for his demise. So, no more whirlwind tours, no more jungles, and no more desert hopping. Torregan will look at anything else he wants to show them, so long as it's not a rainforest."

"When did you…how long have you known?"

"I warned him early on, but when it became official a few days ago I told him immediately. Come on, Althea, don't look at me like that."

"Like what? Like you haven't just ended his life as he's known it?"

"Althea, I usually like to side with my clients, but this time round, I happen to agree with Torregan. Harry has been ill, more than not, the past couple of years. His health has become a life-threatening situation. The sweltering climates and harsh terrains he seems to favor—volcanoes, rainforests, jungles, deserts—this guy doesn't fool around—have taken a toll on his body. Harry is definitely inching closer to the line. Torregan values his life more than the photographs he brings home."

"But he'll get better. I know he will," Althea protested. "He gets better every day."

"Of course he will, honey," Leonel agreed, pressing her hand. "But what about next time? Harry collapsing like that at the airport was a very serious affair. If you hadn't been there to shepherd him, matters could have gone very badly for him. He could have even gone into a coma. You yourself told me that the doctors said he wasn't to even think about leaving the States for at least a year. The long and the short of it is that Harry has to find himself new subject matter to explore and shoot. Look, a new direction won't hurt him any. It will prevent him from getting stale."

Althea was immediately suspicious. "Is that what you're *really* thinking, that he's getting stale?"

Leonel shook his head. "No, sweetie, that was a poor choice of words. That's not what I think, even remotely. Harry is in top form, at his peak, as far as his career is concerned. But look at him. He's been hospitalized three times in the last two years. His body is paying a heavy price for his art. I'm not abandoning him, Althea, I promise. We still have this book to put together, and I'm looking forward to it winning a Pulitzer prize. Aren't you? He sure could use the extra money. I simply want him to be able to walk to the podium to accept the prize."

"No wonder he hasn't returned my calls. He must be upset."

Stretching back in his chair, Leonel crossed his arms over his chest. His features were a study in the philosophical. "Let me tell you something, ladies. The key to success is in reassessing and reestablishing your goals at every turn."

"You mean as in cutting your losses?"

"Something like." He winked.

But Althea was in no mood to be mollified. She was too busy wondering whether Harry's best friend had betrayed him or, in any case, if Harry would think so.

Chapter Thirteen

"I'm coming, I'm coming," Althea shouted over the insistent, piercing ring of the doorbell. Her peach-colored Balenciaga gown swished at her ankles as she hurried across the living room, carrying a bottle of champagne.

Flinging wide the door, she took in Harry's tuxedo and haircut. "Harry, you look gorgeous. You outdid yourself." His hair neatly brushed his collar with elegant style. "Come in, come in. I was just trying to get this stubborn cork out."

Reaching for the wine, Harry smiled. "Here, allow me. This is good champagne you have here. And you're looking very, um—" Harry looked

Althea up and down, to settle on the bodice of her gown "—very, um, showy yourself. I don't suppose I have much say about that."

Biting back her laughter, Althea shook her head. "Harry, I think you just said a mouthful."

"It's all that cleavage," Harry protested as he eyed her ample bosom. "It's one thing to see it in pictures, but a whole other thing to see it in the flesh. I mean, to see *all* that flesh," he added with a rueful smile.

"If you think this gown is revealing, wait till you get to the party."

"Oh, I don't mind looking at other women, I just don't like men looking at mine. Maybe you have a shawl or a hanky, or something? How about a *fichu?* You know, that piece of lace the ladies used to tuck in their bodices in the old days, so their husbands wouldn't get teed off?"

Althea couldn't help the laughter that escaped her glossy red lips. " I don't have a *fichu,* and you are not an irate husband, and this is not the old days. Sounds like you're the only thing *old* around here. *Old-fashioned.*" Locking the door, Althea linked her arm in Harry's and led him to the living room. "Since when did you become such a prude?"

"Since seeing that dress, so don't fault me for trying. Beyond that, you really do look lovely. I can hardly wait to dance with you, wrap my arms around that body," he teased. "But do you think maybe you could forgo slow-dancing with other men? I'm feeling a little possessive tonight."

"Well, since you asked so nicely, I could do that, yes."

"Hmm. Does that mean that if I asked nicely, you would change from that wicked gown to, um, something a little less…nakedy?"

"Nakedy?" Althea grinned. "Did you make up that word?"

"Yeah, but it gets the idea across, doesn't it?" Bending down, he pressed a light kiss to her soft cheek. "I know, I know, don't muss up the makeup, but you smell so good. Here we go," Harry said as he popped the champagne cork, "let's toast the evening. To all the lascivious men I'm going to have to protect you from."

"To bare-naked ladies?" Althea added with a mischievous grin as she settled on the sofa.

"To them, too," Harry retorted.

"Hmm. Come, Harry," she said, patting the spot next to her, "come sit down and tell me what you've been up to, while we have a minute."

Harry sat down, but he was far more interested in nuzzling her neck. She pushed him away with a soft laugh. "Not now, silly. I just took an hour to dress."

"I can reverse that in five minutes," he offered, playing with the strap of her gown. "Two minutes, if you're really rushed." A man of his word, he pressed a kiss to her bare shoulder.

Althea had to smile as she pulled away and adjusted her strap. "The last time we were together, you were mad at me."

"That was then, this is now," Harry announced as he sipped his champagne. "Like you said, we're not seventeen. If there are things you feel you need to do, you said I was crowding you...." Harry shrugged. "Besides," he added, "Leonel gave me a good talking to. He's your best fan, you know. He told me to lay off before I ruined everything."

Althea's eyes twinkled at Harry's left-handed admission, but she would take what she could. He was a hard act. "Thank you, Harry, for that vote of confidence. I really was worried for a while there. You were pretty angry at one point."

"Well, you know me, I have a bad temper. Besides, I have my own problems to straighten out."

"Are you referring to Torregan Publishing not financing your next expedition?"

"That I am," he admitted, visibly annoyed. "Leonel told me you heard the news. I'm still not sure if I've been stabbed in the back. What do you think?"

"Do *you* think Leonel could have done more to save your contract?"

"Nah. I'm just naturally suspicious. Leonel's a good friend. I'm not totally done, you know. Torregan just doesn't want me dropping dead on their watch, is all." He laughed. "I suppose they're right. I have to say, I have never been so sick in my life as the last two months, and I don't think I want to go through that again. I still have moments when I'm really weak and have to lie down. Maybe they're right—I should find a new line of work."

"You don't mean to give up photography, do you?" Althea was horrified at the idea. "I won't let you, I—"

"Calm down, honey," Harry said, draping a comforting arm around her shoulders. "I'm not giving up photography. How can I give up something that is my life? It would be like asking you to give up modeling, wouldn't it? I'm just going to have to find alternative subject matter. It's a big world, not all jungle. I just have to figure it out. Maybe weddings and bar mitzvahs. I hear the money is pretty good."

Althea shot up, but when she saw that he was teasing she punched him playfully on the arm. "You scared me for a minute."

"Okay then, there are all these fashion shoots. There's money in that, too, I've heard."

"I don't know…all those girls coming on to you."

"Yeah," Harry said, wagging his head. "But look on the bright side. I'd be coming home to you every night."

Althea tapped her lips thoughtfully with a carefully polished nail as she played into the fantasy. "Until one day, when you didn't come home.…"

Harry laughed. "And left you with a passel of kids?"

"How many is a passel?"

"I don't know. I'll have to ask Leonel. He knows that sort of stuff. On second thought—" he grinned, his golden head at a jaunty angle "—I suppose we can figure that one out for ourselves, when the time comes. But for now," he announced with a quick look at his watch, "I think we'd better get moving if we're going to this party."

If Althea figured she was the only woman to descend from a Jeep in five-inch, gold-embossed Manolo Blahnik stilettos, she was right, but she didn't mind. Watching Harry drive downtown had been an experience in sensuality. Now that his health had improved, she was beginning to recognize the old, quirky appeal that he held for her, so many years ago. The sprinkle of brown hair on his knuckles, the way his strong hands grasped the wheel, his brow as it furrowed while he concentrated on traffic, the flex of his shoulder when he made a turn. Althea thought she was probably attending the party with the sexiest guy alive. There was nothing like a man in a tux to raise a woman's antennae, and hers had definitely been raised.

Seeing Harry anew made her more hopeful of their relationship. Their unexpected exchange of confidences back in her apartment also reassured her. She liked that he had apologized for rushing her, that he was opening up, sharing his concerns with her. Things had always been easy for him. Maybe his own crisis would soften his rough edges.

Barring the heavy Saturday-night traffic, they were able to arrive at the party at a fashionably late hour. When he handed his keys to the valet and cupped her elbow, Harry intuitively picked up on her distraction.

"Althea, are you all right?"

"Just thinking," she said softly.

Harry gave her a curious, questioning look, but whatever he was going to say was lost in the waiting doorman's smile as he held open the restaurant door. The young couple was swept into the party on the sound of raucous delight, swallowed whole by New York at its most social—dinner, dancing, drinking. Trading confidences was not on the menu.

The party was being held in a hot new restaurant on the outskirts of Greenwich Village. Designed with an Eastern motif, it was resplendent with colorful tile work, artificial minarets, tons of red velvet and a twenty-foot bar that was fast gaining a reputation as the latest hangout for the twenty-something crowd. As it would be, until the next bar opened, in the next restaurant, on the next block. This was New York—restaurants opened and closed in the blink of an eye.

Anyone who was anyone was going to be there, as Althea had warned Harry days before. Now that he was there, Harry thought she was right. The place was too damned crowded, the space too damned small, and he wanted to leave five minutes after they arrived, but watching Althea disappear into the throng, kissing, hugging and laughing like a schoolgirl as she greeted her old friends, he knew he wasn't going anywhere soon. He couldn't help thinking it was a royal waste of time, but he had promised to be nice, so he headed for the bar, ordered a beer and tried to look happy. He barely managed and would have tried harder if he had known that his sullen face was far more interesting to a stranger. The stranger who thought so turned out to be an old enemy.

"Ha. I thought it was you. Harry Bensen, in the flesh."

Harry turned to see who was shouting his name and was caught off guard by a tiny termagant waving an unlit cigarette in his face. Small in stature, she was a force in the industry. Skinny to the point of emaciation, she was dressed to the nines. Her makeup was perfect, her hair arranged in spectacular dreds. Harry was annoyed to see her.

"Jeez, Connie. Now, why am I not surprised to see you?"

Connie Niles smiled at Harry, her wide smile telling him she'd had more than her share of champagne. If she saw his annoyance, though, she was bent on ignoring it. The way she elbowed herself a space beside him at the bar told him she was there for the count. "Happy to see you, too, champ. How's it going, or am I interrupting one of your memorable sulks?" She had fond memories of him, too.

"I'm having the time of my life," Harry snapped, curt to the point of rudeness.

"Yes, I can tell," she said, her voice full of sawdust.

Dipping his head, Harry had the grace to look ashamed. "Want anything?" he asked as he motioned to the bartender for another beer.

"Now, that's more like it," Connie said, leaning into him with a thin smile. "An apple martini would be perfect, thanks. It's my latest form of depravity."

Jarred by her touch, Harry twisted away as far as he could. They didn't speak until the bartender arrived to take their order. But Connie had read his face accurately. "Harry, if you hate this sort of thing, why did you come?"

Harry's mouth was an unpleasant twist. "In a word, Althea. Why else would I waste my time? And you?"

"Whatever are you thinking?" Connie laughed lightly. "I wouldn't miss this party for the world. This *is* my world."

"That's what Althea said," Harry growled.

"Oh, I can see that we are here with bells on our toes," Connie snorted. "Thanks," she said as the bartender slid her drink before her. "Heads up," she crowed, her brown face bright with anticipation.

Harry watched as she sipped from her wide, crystal goblet apparently pleased with the result. Privately he agreed, the beer was good and cold, but for him, the free beer and Althea were the only reasons to be there.

"Well, Bensen, it's been a long time. How have

you been? Up to any good?" Fortified, Connie was ready for conversation.

Harry shrugged as he scanned the room. "Same old, same old. I just got back from Brazil."

"I heard. And ran straight into my little girl at the airport. Talk about karma."

"She's not your little girl, she's not even a girl, and I don't believe in karma," he said irritably.

"Well, I do," Connie said as she held her glass to her lips. "Althea *did* mention that her divorce had become final. You don't waste time, do you, Harry?"

"Our *reunion,* if you even want to call it that, was a complete accident."

"Oh, sure, of course, but what about the second date? Was that an accident, too?"

"Excuse me?" Harry frowned.

But Connie was in no mood to humor him. "What are you doing here, Harry? What are you *really* doing here? Guarding your property?"

"Althea is not my property," he growled, his temper—and his beer—beginning to get the best of him.

"Yeah, like you were the only available male in the phone book." Connie laughed, but her brown eyes were insolent. "Tell me, Bensen, does Althea know how much you love attending these parties?"

"Connie, lighten up. I don't know how *I* feel."

"Oh, I think you know *exactly* how you feel," Connie said, sweeping the room with her cynical eyes. "The photographers, all the dirty old men, the

kissy kissy stuff. The surfeit of skin. The booze."
Waving her glass, she made known to the bartender
her need for a refill.

Connie had it right. Harry hated the whole scene,
he hated the modeling industry. He watched, nau-
seous as Althea was cornered by a journalist with a
gold pen and a spiral notebook. Harry raged, as he
followed the direction of the journalist's eyes. How
could Althea stand it? Connie's harsh, grating voice
answered that question, and they came easily now
she was tipsy.

"It doesn't look like our girl is going to have any
trouble getting back into the grind, does it? Actually,
this is the good part of a dirty business. It's all about
publicity, you know. Being seen and all that. But
Althea knows this," she said, watching her favorite
model evade the clever hands of the journalist.
"She's good. She knows how to handle things."

"Does Althea know in what high esteem you hold
your clients?" Harry asked morosely.

"Althea is having a good time. That's what she
knows. Like I said, she wasn't born yesterday, she
knows what's up. I'm in the business of selling faces.
She has a face, so I sell it, and make her gobs of
money while I'm at it. End of subject."

"She can do better," Harry muttered.

"Sure she can," Connie said agreeably. "And so
can you. Or are we talking about two different
things?" She laughed loudly, as the martinis began

to take effect. "Yeah, I always thought you were too weighty for my princess."

"Too white, you mean."

"That, too, Sir Galahad. But weighty, also, wanting to save the world, taking life too seriously. You never were a party animal, were you? Harry, you know what your trouble is?"

"Please, don't keep me in suspense."

"There you have it. You never mastered the art of small talk, Bensen." She was smiling, but Harry could detect her irritation as she tossed her head Althea's way. "Look at her, she's stunning, she lights up the room. Are you going to take that away from her?"

Harry stared into the gilded mirror that embellished the bar, reflecting back the crowded room. There must have been two hundred people crowding the dance floor—designers and models, movie stars, journalists, wannabes of all types. Strobe lights added to the madcap euphoria, making the music seem louder and the air thicker than it really was. And in the middle of the madness, Althea dancing, wildly, her head thrown back as she moved to the music, her slender body gleaming with the faint sheen of sweat. She charmed the crowd, her excitement irresistible, and Harry watched her rake in their adoration. Connie was right. Althea was back in form, as if she had never left. He felt depressed.

"You poor lovesick bantling," Connie said, patting his arm. "You really care for her, don't you?"

Harry looked as if he were trying to choose the right answer, but in the end he just shrugged. Connie let him off the hook for the sake of Althea, who had managed to make her way to their side. Snatching an hors d'oeuvre from the silver tray of a passing waiter, Althea eyed them suspiciously as she popped a mushroom into her mouth. She knew there was no love lost at this end of the bar.

"Hey, guys, what's up?"

Connie's smile was blissful, and Harry knew it had a lot to do with apple martinis, but he remained silent. He didn't say a word, either, when Connie put her hand on his forearm for the sake of emphasis.

"Harry and I are getting reacquainted, darling. It's been years. So much has happened. All that churning water under all those rusty bridges."

Althea was skeptical. If two people couldn't care less about each other, it was these two. And Harry definitely did not look too happy about that hand resting on his arm. Still, she didn't see any blood. "Harry, want to dance?"

It was a slow dance. Harry nodded and led her to the dance floor.

"What was that all about?" Althea asked as she slipped into his arms.

"Hush." Harry sighed. "I've been waiting all night for this moment."

"Me, too," she whispered as she rested her cheek on his chest, everything else suddenly forgotten. The feel of Harry's warm hands on the small of her back was the only thing she could think of. Even the photographers snapping away didn't disturb her.

Then they were home and Harry was fumbling with the lock to her door, unable to find the right key. Althea watched him thoughtfully for a long moment, until her face filled with a radiant light. "Harry."

"Hold on, I'll get it, just give me another minute. Too much champagne…beer…"

"Harry!"

"You know, if you didn't have so many damned keys on one chain I—"

"Harry, let's make love."

Harry was so shocked he dropped the entire key ring. "What? What? I…um…could you repeat that?"

"Harry!"

Suddenly the aftereffects of the wine were gone. "I heard, sweetheart," he said quietly. "It's just that I was expecting you to say something else."

"Like what?"

"Like anything else!" he said with a faint smile. The eyes that pinned her were serious, but the soft lips that suddenly covered hers were the flight of a butterfly. She thought he was going to speak, he seemed about to, but Harry only drew her into the fold of his arms and rested his cheek on her head.

Relaxing into his embrace, Althea wrapped her arms about his waist and buried her face against his chest. How nice he smelled, all male and starched linen. She could have stood that way forever. What took her so long *to know?* How odd *to know,* in the span of a moment, that this man was right for her, that *he* was the man who completed her. Wordlessly, she backed from his grasp to reclaim her keys. Reaching for his hand, she pressed a kiss to his palm. "These hands can work a different kind of magic."

Entering her apartment, Althea dropped her keys in a bowl, abandoned her wrap on the sofa and led them into her bedroom.

"You don't waste time," Harry observed, looking around the room he had long been forbidden.

"We're too old for the couch, don't you think?"

"Oh, I do, I do! That was *not* meant as criticism. But—" Looking over the huge bed covered with an army of pink pillows, Harry shook his head, a crooked smile on his lips. "Couldn't get much girlier than that, I'm thinking. All that lace might cramp my style."

Kicking off her shoes, Althea pressed a shy kiss to his mouth. "I doubt it."

Her bluntness made him smile. Gathering her into his arms, Harry pulled her close, his breath a fan against her cheek. "Althea, Althea. My beautiful princess." His whisper was nearly a prayer. Exulting in the moment, wanting to savor it, Harry cupped her face with his long fingers. His lips a hairsbreath from hers, his tongue rimmed her mouth, the taste of her better than any wine he'd drank this evening.

"Are you sure? I wouldn't want this night to be the champagne talking. There's still time to change your mind."

"Harry, I stopped drinking hours ago."

"And I may never drink again," he swore, skimming her arms with the lightest touch. Slipping the straps from her shoulders, the creamy slope of her breast bared to his hungry eyes, he cupped her, almost virginal in his exploration. "What gift is this?" he teased, but his whisper was reverent.

He meant it, too. She had unlocked her heart, but unwittingly made *him* her prisoner. Every touch meant to make her shudder had an equal effect on him. He wondered if she could tell, if she could feel his heart beating wildly, feel the passion he fought to contain, the challenge she made to his senses.

But he didn't want to ask, didn't want to hear the sound of his voice, or hers, not unless it was the purr of pleasure. He told her this when he captured her mouth in a kiss hungry and hard. He needed to move— suddenly he was impatient to love her. Suddenly he wanted her naked beneath him. With an urgency that surprised him, he began to nibble at her earlobe, plant rough kisses on her neck, discover how sensitive she was to his fingertips as they explored the curves of her spine. His breath, warm and moist on the cusp of her shoulder, was an electric shock intended to flood her with sensation, an assault against a decade of defense. One by one, he felt her defences come down.

"Do you like this?"

"Oh, yes," she breathed as his moist lips found the tiny pulse in her throat.

"And this?"

"I like," she murmured as his thumb skimmed the satin bodice of her gown.

"This, too?"

"Oh, yes!"

Stirred by his onslaught, Althea slid her hands beneath Harry's jacket to sweep it from his shoulders. Half done, she lost interest and began to unbutton his shirt. His tie had been lost long ago. One by one, as Harry's mouth explored the hollow of her neck, Althea bared his skin, laughing as his furry chest, flat brown nipples and sculpted belly were revealed. "You are so beautiful, Harry, I think I must have done something very special in another life to have found you."

"Hey, missy, you're stealing my lines. Althea, honey, I have dreamed of this way too many times, that's a fact."

They were not children fumbling in the back seat of a car. Unzipping her gown, she let it slide to her ankles, leaving herself covered with only the tiniest wisp of silk. "You have me."

Swallowing hard, Harry flung off his own clothes, not caring where they landed. Her arms outstretched, Althea beckoned him down to the bed, drew him between her long legs, his weight carefully balanced above her. *Long legs, slender arms, full breasts.* Harry's laughing eyes were full of humor. "Allie, honey, you make me feel like a bumbling school-boy."

Althea stretched like a cat under his admiring glance, her hands thrumming the hard muscles of his arms as they balanced above her. "I think you're doing fine."

"My goddess," he breathed, but words beyond that were impossible for Harry. Their tongues performed a slow waltz that only they could dance—he infinitely preferred to kiss her. Her lips tasted of honey and champagne—all the bubbles uncorked—and his tongue darted forward to taste every bit of her.

"Open for me, Althea." Desire raging through his body, his tongue thrust forward to part her lips. He explored her mouth with impunity, hardly allowing her to catch her breath.

"Harry," she gasped with a ragged laugh. "I can't breathe!"

Harry smiled and eased away, but he was back the moment she caught her breath, his need for her all-consuming. His forehead sheened with a light sweat, he crossed the line from desire to passion. When Althea understood this, she gave way to her own.

"You don't have to wait," she heard herself say.

"Good, because I don't think I can." A gentle delving of his artful fingers to make sure she was ready, and Harry's hips met hers. His muscles coiled beneath her damp palms as he strained to maintain control. His body, slick with sweat, swayed above her for one last moment, the time it took for her to cover him with a condom.

"Althea!" It was a prayer he breathed once more as he slid into her, his heart hammering wildly. He took her in a swift, hard thrust—it was that easy, his response to her was so powerful.

And so was hers. They came together, unsure who cried out first, equally shattered by the unexpected power of their encounter.

"Harry," Althea gasped, his head heavy on her heaving bosom, "was it always like this?"

"I'm not sure," he barely managed to answer.

Harry wasn't sure of anything except to wonder if he had just made the mistake of his life. As soon as it hit Althea what just happened—fireworks and cannons exploding—she might book the next flight to Birmingham. Pretending to fall asleep, he threw his leg across her hips and burrowed his nose in her hair.

But Althea wasn't having it.

"Harry."

Harry's eyes shot wide, the picture of innocence. "Hmm?"

Althea's look was nine shades of sardonic. One thing she hated more than a sleepy lover was a remorseful one. "I'm hungry."

Not the response he was looking for. But perhaps

better than he'd hoped. Harry shot up and smiled. "I know a great diner. Breakfast is on me." He was gone, sparing only the time it took to cover her with a blanket.

Listening to the shower run, Althea let her thoughts wander. It seemed there was more danger living in New York than Paris, and the risk was called Harry Bensen. Drifting on uncharted currents in the wake of her divorce, Harry Bensen was a riptide she hadn't been expecting. Not wanting to make any decisions, not sure what her choices even were, she had allowed Harry to coax her back into his heart. Now *she* had coaxed *him* to bed.

And there had been nothing delicate about their lovemaking. It had been passionate, hot, sweaty love between cool cotton sheets. A direct contrast to the spare, cold kisses of her ex-husband. Harry had been a totally involved lover, that was it, while Daniel had held himself aloof, almost a spectator. But Harry's passion notwithstanding, he was nervous, she could sense it in the way he'd run for cover in the shower. Oh, Lord, was he having second thoughts?

"Harry?"

Emerging from the steamy bathroom, a towel wrapped around his midriff, she thought he was the sexiest man she had ever seen.

"Seen my underwear anywhere?" he asked, trying to sort out the clothes spread every which way across the room.

"Harry!"

"Yo."

Leaning up on an elbow, Althea smiled. "Slow down! Just in case you're worried, I'm not going to have a tantrum. I wouldn't be sitting here if I were."

Harry's sigh of relief was audible as he perched beside her on the tangled sheets. "I can't tell you how glad I am to hear that! I was having a bad case of nerves back there in the shower."

"I wondered why you were taking so long."

"Well, I knew you enjoyed yourself." Harry frowned. "I was just worried that you might regret it."

"No regrets in this corner." Althea grinned. "But I don't want you to think I do this sort of thing as a habit. Jump into bed at the least inclination, I mean."

Slipping on a pair of khakis, Harry zipped up, then bent over the pillow to plant a hard kiss on Althea's lips. "Honestly, I didn't think you did."

"Ooh, are you saying that I wasn't noticeably… *experienced?*"

"Whoa! I'm not saying anything near. It was great. I thought I was going to die from sheer bliss!"

"Well, then…" Wrapping her arms around his neck, she pressed her mouth to his. "Give me a few minutes to catch my breath and I'll be ready again."

Chapter Fourteen

Two days later Althea reported to her first shoot in more than two years. Waking to a serious case of nerves, she struggled into the sassiest jeans in her closet, put on the highest-heeled boots she owned and glossed her pouty mouth with the reddest lipstick in her makeup drawer. The chuck wagon was lifting its awning when she arrived at the site, the aroma of fresh coffee floating on the cool morning air. Helping herself to a cup—black, no sugar—and a small bowl of fresh fruit, she entered the studio and found a stool on which to perch, careful to keep out of the way as the film crew slowly but methodically set up their equipment. She was just finishing the last chunk of pineapple when the shoot director came over to say hello.

"Althea Almott, I'm so glad you could be here!" he exclaimed.

"Hello, Frank."

"When I called Connie last week, I had no idea you would be available. I didn't even know you were back in the States. Silly me, not reading the papers, right? About your divorce and all," he said. "But who's got time? I have been just so busy. And now *you,* here. Landing the great Almott, well, how lucky can I be, I ask you?"

"Thanks, Frank." Irritating and effusive, he went on and on, but Althea was not about to interrupt the director. Thankfully, she was summoned to the makeup trailer. Excusing herself, she slid from the stool and headed for the trailer.

"Maybe we can catch up on the news over lunch, darling?" she heard him call.

Sending him a thumbs-up, she made a silent vow to make herself scarce in between shots. Frank was buddy-buddy with some very powerful gossip columnists. She could almost guarantee the headlines of anything she told him, even in confidence.

It took an hour to get her makeup just right, Althea having strong opinions about what constituted "just right." She had a well-earned reputation for perfection. After she was She-Laqued, she was steered to the wardrobe trailer, where she and the wardrobe mistress discussed dresses and accessories. After much discussion, they settled on a pale-green ensemble. While the gown was being steamed, her nails were painted a complementary color and eye shadow applied to match. The hair stylist stood by, discussing hairdos while the shoe mistress came to apologize but she only had size eights. Althea sighed, but said nothing, having spent many an afternoon scrunched into a shoe far too small for her long, narrow, size-nine feet. She was sitting, a towel around her neck as her curls were highlighted, when a spectacular blonde in a bright-blue gown passed by.

"I know you. You're Althea Almott. Or you used to be, before you got married."

"I still am Althea Almott. I married but never gave up my professional name," she said genially.

The young woman—could she be all of seventeen?—nodded agreeably. "Yes, I think you're right. You never know what the future will bring, do you? One day a superstar, the next day a divorcee."

Althea looked at the girl sharply, to see if her fangs were showing. No, her tiny, white teeth seemed perfectly even, and there was no blood dripping that she could see. The blond-haired girl stared back, her blue gaze wide-eyed and level, so young she had yet to learn good manners. Althea watched as she flicked her long, silky hair over her shoulder and strolled away. It was a message Althea could not help but read, so transparent she had to bite her lip to keep from laughing.

Working until late afternoon under the hot lights, Althea found she had become unused to the heat. The klieg lights seemed hotter than ever, and the prop crew had been unable to secure enough fans to cool things down. Thus the makeup artists stood guard with face powder and tissue, ready to brush anyone who dared to sweat. She had to fight to quell the nausea that rose up, protesting her dehydration. Whereas once she might have called the shoot to a halt until she revived, she was reluctant to do so now, nervous that she held no sway.

The photographer, new and desperate to establish himself in the business, seemed to be doing it at everyone's expense. Barking orders, changing the shoot sequence, disparaging everyone's clothes, he created an inordinate amount of tension on the set. Everyone either cringed when he passed or gobbled aspirin by the handful. Frank had already corrected her twice on the way she was holding her head, and the cameraman continually complained that he had to readjust the lights to address the complexity of her skin tones. The blond girl watched her so closely from the camera's edge that Althea wondered if she was spying for someone. Who that might be she had no idea, and she berated herself for being paranoid, but her uneasiness grew.

She had been gone too long. She no longer had the edge. It belonged to the blond—and the brunettes and redheads—everyone who had come up the ranks while she, Althea, had been in Europe on an overlong honeymoon with a man who hadn't even cared for her.

Oh, my.

She went home a rag that night, kicked off her shoes and collapsed on the sofa. The phone machine blinked red, but she had no heart to talk and fell asleep where she was. Waking in the dead of night, she dragged herself off to bed, too tired to even make dinner.

The next day was no better, perhaps even more of a strain. Whereas the blond woman was nowhere in sight, a young brown-skinned woman decided the sisterhood allowed her entrée to Althea's privacy. Cornering Althea during the lunch break, she dropped into the folding chair beside her, showing only slightly more tact than yesterday's blonde. Eyeing Althea's chicken salad, she sighed dramatically.

"I wish I could eat like that, but I swear, these hips put on pounds just drinking water."

Suddenly Althea's sandwich tasted like cardboard. Putting it down, she waited for the girl to continue.

"Oh, please," the young woman protested. "Don't stop eating on my account. You look like you could eat anything."

Althea looked at her in silence, amazed at the girl's forwardness. Had she missed something, the way all these youngsters were carrying on, or had she just missed *herself* in the details. Was it her? Them?

Time? What was missing? And why did she feel so powerless to deal with their careless insults?

She thought about it off and on the rest of the day, and tried to sort things out on the way home. None too successful, she was cheered by the sight of Harry sitting in her lobby. "Hello, Harry." She smiled wanly.

He couldn't possibly miss the exhaustion written on her face, but wisely, he ignored it. "Not answering your phones, these days?" he asked instead, as he rose to his feet.

"I barely have the energy."

"Save it. I was never one for small talk. Come on, let's go upstairs." Grabbing her satchel, he headed for the elevator. "I brought us some steaks," he said, explaining the shopping bag in his other hand. "And lady, you definitely look like you could use some red meat."

"You think that a good steak, medium rare, is the answer to all mankind's problems. But actually, I could use a home-cooked meal," she agreed, surprised how glad she was to see him.

Entering the apartment, Althea flicked on the lights and kicked off her shoes. She made no protest when Harry ordered her off to take a shower while he began to rattle pots and pans. By the time she was toweling her hair, he was lounging in the doorway of the steamy bathroom, nursing an icy glass of Chardonnay.

The thick terrycloth towel loosely wrapped about

her made for all sorts of interesting fantasies, *all* of which involved its removal, but Harry restrained himself, content to watch as Althea battled with her wet curls and finally clipped them to the top of her head. Watching her do something so ordinary made him feel closer to her, as if they were bound in a family way. Funny, he thought, how something so commonplace could suddenly be so appealing, when all these years he had avoided these situations. He'd heard that the heart marched to its own drummer, and supposed now that it was true. His own heart was murmuring *marriage, family, kids.* He wondered how she would take the news.

"Seen enough?" Althea asked, interrupting his reveries with a quiet question. Her eyes twinkling, she dropped her towel to the floor.

Harry choked on his wine, the dazzling sight of her brown body revealed so unexpectedly a shock to his nervous system. Suddenly he was standing taller, his face flushed, his body on full alert.

Encouraged by the awestruck look in his eyes, Althea reached for the wineglass cradled in his fist— he probably didn't even remember he was holding it—and placed it gently on the rim of the marble sink. Standing tiptoe, she slid her arms about his neck and pressed her mouth to his ear. "I adore you, Harry Bensen," she whispered, her breath tickling his collarbone.

Intoxicated, Harry leaned on the doorjamb for

support. "Althea, you're killing me," he breathed, the heat of her pillowy breasts burning through the thin cotton of his shirt.

"Yes, and you're loving it," he heard her whisper as her hand slid down to fiddle with the zipper of his pants.

Lord, how could six inches of metal take *so* long to unfasten? He wondered, but slowly, gratefully, he felt it give way. *Ah, that's it, that's fine, no, that's wonderful,* he sighed when her hand *finally* covered his bulging groin.

He tried to stay upright, but the way she was torturing him, it was no mean feat to keep his balance. He closed his eyes on the exquisite pain she caused him, her tiny tongue flicking at his ear, her fingers tugging the buttons of his shirt. Dipping her hand beneath the fabric, he felt her long nails lightly score his nipples. When *did* she learn to do this stuff?

"Allie, we have *got* to get to the bed!"

"Hmm, yes, yes."

But he could tell she wasn't listening. He tried to temper his response. If he didn't, he would embarrass himself any minute. "I missed you, Allie. The day you left was agony."

That caught her attention, but Althea only laughed. "Harry, it's been all of four days!"

"A long four days," he told her, his blue eyes wide and serious. "When you didn't answer my calls, I thought the worst."

"You always think the worst. You're a regular pessimist. Hmm, you smell so good," she said, pressing her nose to his throat. "You smell just like a man."

"Well, that's good," Harry allowed gratefully, but she took his words away with a smothering, slow kiss. The world spun on an axis of their own making until she pulled back on a sigh. A satisfied look deepened the color of Harry's blue eyes. "Oh, and by the way, don't think I didn't notice this little band of gold around your neck."

Althea's face grew hot as she toyed with the ring dangling from the chain. "Don't smile like that. I decided that you meant well, and I came to enjoy the idea of wearing it. Like you said, it's not an engagement ring. But I do want things to be different between us, this time around. Wearing your ring sort of fit in with that idea."

Lowering her mouth to his, her kiss was a tender avowal that underscored her words. There was a quality to her kiss that told him she really cared. The look in her eyes, when she raised her head, seemed to ask if he felt the same way. Unable to speak, Harry buried his face in her neck. His arms about her tired body spoke for him. "Althea, let's move to the bedroom. I don't think we have much time left for foreplay. To think you were bone tired only a minute ago!" he teased. Harry's fingers found their way to the strong muscles of her smooth, firm tush, his touch delicate as he explored her warm curves, her quiet moan of delight exquisite encouragement.

Althea could hardly speak for the distraction he was posing. Tucking her body into the shelter of his, her head dropped to his shoulder and she gave herself up to the intimacy of his touch. "I missed you, too, Harry," she admitted. "Terribly."

Harry's eyes spoke his relief as he pressed his mouth to hers. His kiss was soft and she quivered at the tenderness he showed. But then he was not so tender, his lips smothering hers as he trapped her in the iron grip of his arms and led them to the bedroom.

His hands circling her hips, he clasped her body, lifting her higher. Her heart thumping, the musky scent of his body beguiling, Althea implored him with her eyes to stop his teasing. Harry understood and laughed, but with a swift, gentle roll, he was looming over her, suddenly serious. No more sweet kisses. Flesh against flesh, he plunged into her, his wild exhilaration meeting her own. "Tell me how much you want me, Allie. Tell me that it's good." The tendons of his neck taut, his arms corded with tension, Harry braced himself as Althea quickened with surprise.

"Wait!" he cried, feeling her involuntary tremors, but he knew it was too late, that she had traveled to another place. Her orgasm was so galvanizing, he couldn't help but follow. The electric shock that jolted her body passed to his, sapping his willpower. Freed by his uncontrollable passion, Harry surrendered to the liquid fire that scorched him, thrusting into her again and again until he shattered into a million golden stars.

My God, what was that? But Harry did not say those words. Conversation was beyond him. Breathing was beyond him. He collapsed in the cradle of Althea's arms, sure he would never move again.

Leaning back against the pillows, basking in the afterglow of their lovemaking, Harry played with Althea's hand. Pressing her palm to his lips, twice he started to speak, but sheer exhaustion stopped him each time. *She* didn't seem to notice as she scrambled from bed.

"I'm starving," she announced with forthright humor as she found her robe. "Come on, lazybones, let's eat that delicious dinner you were making before...um...*before*...and then you can sleep."

"Jeez, Althea, where'd you get your second wind?" he asked, still weak from their lovemaking.

Althea laughed as she threw the blankets to the floor. "Great sex gives me energy." She grinned. "I wish I could say the same for you, old man!" Laughing as he pulled himself up with a groan, she wrapped herself in a blue velvet bathrobe. "And I've got to get some sleep soon. This has been the week from hell."

"Any particular reason?" he said as he searched under the bed for his boxers.

"I'm still trying to figure it out. At first, I thought it was the new-girl-on-the-block syndrome, but I'm beginning to wonder if it's simply just me—my history and all. Oh, well, it's probably just nerves. Give me another week and it'll pass. There are probably too many things going on. Daniel called last night, too."

"Your husband called again?"

"My *ex*-husband called again," she corrected him with a mischievous grin.

"Sorry. Right. I wondered why you didn't answer your cell phone."

"Oh, no you don't, Harry. That had nothing to do with Daniel calling. You called pretty late, and I was sleeping. That's the long and the short of it, my friend."

Harry wasn't sure whether to believe her but decided not to let his jealousy get the better of him. Especially after having made love the last hour. "Okay." He shrugged.

"Harry."

"Okay, okay, I believe you. Then what *did* Mr. *ex*-husband Ambassador want?"

"Oh, he was going on about this and that, trying to boss me around. You'd think, now that we're divorced, he'd be less inclined to meddle, but he's so used to having his finger in every dish—or is it 'spoon in every pot'? Whatever. I told him to save it for the conference table. These overbearing men!"

"Excuse me?" asked Harry, raising his eyebrows, but Althea had already left the bedroom.

"I didn't think you'd want to eat in the dining room," he explained as he followed her down the hall. I always liked your kitchen, anyway. Yellow and white. Sunny. I'd like to do something like this in my own house."

Looking down at the table set with salad and garlic bread, Althea told him he could copy the whole house if he fed her like this. He put their steaks to sizzle in the broiler and microwaved a couple of potatoes while Althea seasoned the salad.

"Have some, it's great. Spring mix, my favorite. And grape tomatoes. You went all out, didn't you?" she observed as she plopped one in Harry's mouth.

"It's the balsamic vinegar," he agreed as he began to slice up some mushrooms. "I read about it in a cookbook."

Horrified, she watched him drop gobs of butter in the frying pan. "Harry, if you're going to fry those mushrooms," she chided him, "I don't want to begin to count the calories in this meal."

"Don't worry. You can afford it."

"Maybe this once! But not too often mind."

Over dessert, a sugarless strawberry sorbet, Althea began to feel more human. "You're looking better, too," she said, waving her spoon in his direction.

"More human?" he teased.

"I wouldn't go that far." She smiled. "But Leonel said you needed more rest, and he was right."

"I don't know how much rest I'm getting," Harry declared as he pushed aside his plate, "but he certainly is keeping me housebound. I suppose that's okay, since the weather's been so lousy. He loaded me down with the final proof of the book. And now he's pushing me to complete the paperwork for that Pulitzer submission, so I've been pretty busy. In between naps and doctor visits," he added ruefully.

"But no more traveling?"

"No, but I think we've found a compromise. I'd like to talk to you about it. I'll clean up later. Come to bed and I'll tell you all about it." Scraping back their chairs, they headed down the hall.

"Harry?" Althea murmured, half-asleep as she crawled beneath the covers. "That was the best meal I've ever had."

"Yeah, probably because your bed was ten feet away."

"Maybe," she said, curling up around him, her head resting on his chest. She rubbed her cheek against his chest, her hand roaming his belly. "You are a very sexy man," she whispered. "Have I told you that, lately?"

"It's the steak. You love me for my steak."

"That, too."

"Althea…"

"Yes, I'm listening," she promised as her eyes began to droop. "But I have to tell you right now that I have an early call and you can't imagine how many eyes watch me punch the clock, even if it's only figuratively."

Thinking he must be the luckiest man alive to be able to share her bed, Harry lay his head next to Althea's, her hair a fan beneath his cheek as they shared a pillow. "Are you still being spied on?" he asked as he played with her curls.

"Don't laugh." Althea smiled, as she slid her arm beneath her head. "I thought I was imagining it, but Connie Niles was right. All the young models are watching me like hawks, waiting for me to screw up the shoot, or even better, to rip my dress seam. They even watch what I eat. Thank goodness they didn't catch me at dinner tonight. How did they ever get so thin?"

"Anorexia, anyone?"

"Perhaps," Althea murmured as her eyes began to close.

"Allie, if everything is as you say and is so harsh, why are you doing this?"

As if hit with cold water, Althea sat up sharply. "What are you talking about? This is my chance to make it big."

"But you *are* big. You're world famous."

"Oh, Harry," she said, falling back against the pillow, "I *was* big. *Was.* I've been away from the camera so long, and now this divorce… And the competition is ferocious. Have you seen that gorgeous model from Bulgaria—where on earth is Bulgaria, anyway? But it's exciting, too. I love being back in front of the camera. One or two more big jobs and you'll see, I'll be back on top—I mean the *very* top, bigger than I ever was before. Did I mention that Connie stopped by the set this morning to tell me that she had three more jobs lined up? One is in Morocco. Do you believe I've never been to Morocco? She said it was a swimsuit gig but I told her I didn't care what it was, just so long as I was working. Ooh, I am so tired. But here I am running my mouth off and it was you who wanted to talk."

Stretched beside her, Harry watched Althea's eyes close. "Never mind," he said quietly, leaning back against his pillow to stare at the ceiling, "you get some rest. It's nothing that can't wait. Just some stuff that I've been throwing around with Leonel. He was thinking that we—"

But Althea was asleep. Harry watched her, drawing her into the shelter of his arms when she shifted. He loved this woman, he knew that now. He wanted them to spend the rest of their lives together, but how to convince her of the rightness of that? That their love was a good thing, overcoming any problem: the color line, her workload, his illness. It felt good, and something that felt so good could not possibly be wrong. Could it?

Chapter Fifteen

One of the coup jobs Connie had captured for Althea was to walk down the runway for Vera Wang, February Fashion Week. That was the week all the big-name fashion designers showed off their fall clothing lines in New York. Her commercial shoot completed, Althea headed for Bryant Park the next morning, to fulfill her obligation at the fashion tent. She arrived in the middle of a rip-roaring argument between two prima donna hairdressers, the shrieks of a designer screaming for his seamstress, the unexplained absence of a key model, and a florist delivering twenty-five floral arrangements and did anyone know where they went? The chaos was so organized it could stop a clock. Not that anyone sitting out front in the audience would ever know.

The gown Althea was assigned to wear was a breathtaking floor-length evening gown, a cream-colored chiffon with the palest green appliqué across the bodice. Her hair was dressed *big,* that was the word this year, *big,* so that her dark, thick curls rippled over her shoulders and down her back. She received a standing ovation, and later Vera told her it was as much for her return to the catwalk as for the justice she did to the clothes. The camera flashes wove a nonstop spell of celebrity, and when she arrived backstage, people could not help coming up to her with hugs of congratulations. Connie Niles applauded the loudest from her front-row seat and sent Althea home with a dozen roses to celebrate her official return to modeling.

Having decided to skip that evening's parties in favor of a hot shower, Althea had just finished combing out her wet hair when the doorbell rang. It was about time Harry showed up. She sure hoped he had brought something good to eat because she was starving. But she sure wished he would use the key she gave him. The way he was jabbing at the bell was downright annoying.

"Hold your horses, for goodness' sake," she called as she unlocked the dead bolt. "You're going to wake the whole building with all that noise this time of night." Smiling happily, she opened the door. Her face fell as she raised her eyes. The tallest black man she had ever known, the brightest star on the African-American flag—Ambassador Daniel Sheridan Boylan—stood filling her doorway, his handsome, rugged face reflecting a thin-lipped smile as he stood there, amused by her surprise.

"Daniel?" she gasped. Her hand flew to her wildly beating breast. "Daniel?"

"Hello, Althea." Daniel Sheridan Boylan, America's ambassador to France, stood tall, filling the entry with his bigger-than-life presence, his brown eyes mocking. "Were you expecting someone else?"

Althea searched for something to say. Failing that, she stood there gaping, hoping he was an apparition. He was not. He was very much flesh and bone.

"Aren't you going to invite me in?" he asked, his voice as husky as ever. Too many long-winded speeches, she once teased him.

"I...um... Of course. Come in." She gulped and stepped aside to let him pass. Closing the door, she leaned against it for support. "My goodness, you are the last person I expected to see." She smiled faintly.

"Who was the first?" Daniel asked, never one to mince words.

"It was a figure of speech," Althea said evasively as she took his coat. "It *is* almost eleven o'clock, you know."

She was talking to the empty air. While she hung Daniel's coat in the closet, he was making himself at home in the living room, his head practically in the liquor cabinet. "It's been a hell of a long day," he explained as he poked around among the bottles.

Objection was fruitless. Daniel would do as he liked, and if he wanted a drink, he would have one. It was easier to curl up on the sofa and watch the show. "Ah, nothing but the best," he approved as he held up a bottle of Chivas Regal. "Thank goodness that much hasn't changed. I've been looking forward to this drink all night."

"None for me, thanks," she grumbled when he didn't bother to ask. Some things never changed. Certainly not his taste for fine whisky. And fancy clothes. The pin-striped suit he wore was its usual perfect fit; the shine of his shoes was faultless; his taste in ties, impeccable. All as usual. The man didn't know how to spell denim, much less wear it. He had never favored casual clothing, not even when he traveled. Khakis and sneakers were not in his line. Here it was almost eleven o'clock on a winter's night, and Daniel looked as if he was going to a board meeting. Very likely, he had just come from one.

"Did you just fly in from Paris? What brings you to New York?" she heard herself ask, her voice an unfamiliar croak, reeling as she still was at his unannounced appearance.

"You. Do you mind?" he asked, as he made himself comfortable beside her. It was a rhetorical question, asked for politeness' sake. He didn't expect an answer. On the contrary, he loosened his tie, laid it neatly over the arm of the sofa and opened the top two buttons of his silk shirt. Propping his feet on a footstool, he took a sip of his drink. "Single-malt whisky, nectar from the gods." Daniel sighed. Half smiling, he sank back against the sofa and closed his eyes.

"Make yourself comfortable," she muttered.

"Thanks, I don't mind if I do." Daniel grinned, his eyes still closed. "But to be honest, I wasn't exactly in New York."

Daniel's odd segue confused Althea but she knew he wouldn't bother to explain until he was ready. She felt like a second-string actress in a bit comedy, with the added insult of no lines to speak—and he was the director, producer and chief actor, but the audacious moment gave her the opportunity to examine her ex-husband for the first time in months. There were new lines to tally around his eyes, and his mouth pulled down ever so slightly. Perhaps he had not been as untouched by their divorce as she thought. Althea scowled. He looked far too much like a husband just then, and she was feeling too much like a wife.

"You know, the place looks exactly the same as last time I saw it."

Small mercies! He had seen fit to stay awake!

"And as comfortable, too," he continued as he sipped his scotch. "Anyhow, I was in Washington for a meeting and decided on impulse to drive up and say hello."

"Some impulse," Althea snorted. "Washington is a five-hour drive, last time I heard."

"My driver is very good."

"And you pay him a lot."

"And I pay him a lot." Daniel smiled agreeably. "As it happens, I don't get back to the States that often, you know that, and I really did want to see how you were getting on. I was...*concerned.*"

Althea's mouth dropped. "*You* were worried about *me?* I don't believe it."

"Believe. The way you left without a word, I had to hire a private detective just to make sure you were all right."

"What a waste of time and money. Why didn't you just ask me?"

"I wasn't sure if I could trust you to tell me the truth. Whenever we spoke, you were so uncommunicative. No matter what you think, Althea, I do have your welfare in mind."

Althea was amused. "For heaven's sake, Daniel, we were just divorced. What did you expect, wine and roses?"

Daniel's eyes swept her with approval. "You do look good. Tell me, then, since I did drive all the way up here to ask, how exactly are you?"

"I am fine," she said, enunciating each word. "Very fine. I just did the catwalk this afternoon for

Vera Wang. I can't ask for more. And last week I shot a commercial, so things are going pretty well, workwise."

"I'm glad," he said, raising his glass to his lips. "You seemed so distraught the last time I saw you."

"Oh, for pity's sake, Daniel," Althea said, rolling her eyes, "did you think I was suicidal or something? Oh, my, you did."

"Don't be ridiculous. Of course I didn't," Daniel said tersely. "You still have a difficult time taking me at my word, don't you? I told you, I simply needed to see for myself that you were managing."

"*Managing,* hmm? Daniel, you always did have a way with words. Well, here I am," she said, flinging her arms wide. "Managing about as well as can be expected, considering."

Daniel shook his head. "Considering what? Come on, honey, did you really think we should continue playing house, given the circumstances?"

Althea found that a difficult question to answer. She wished she was able to tell him that if he had been more forthcoming, they might not have landed in the mess they did. But he had always been an enigma, too much the diplomat. Used to hiding his cards, he hid them from his own wife, and she had trained herself not to ask. Then it was too late.

"Althea?" Daniel woke her from her reverie. "I came to make peace with you, not to argue."

"Please, Daniel, spare me the melodrama. Save it

for the conference tables. Have you nothing to say for *yourself*?"

Daniel sat forward, his elbows on his knees as he rolled his glass between his palms. His sidelong glance was sorrowful. "Are you asking me if I miss you? Damn well, I do. It was nice to have a woman around, to be coddled, to have my feet massaged at midnight."

"That's not what I meant," Althea said with a withering stare that made him laugh.

"Come on, Althea, haughty doesn't become you. I know what you meant, but that's all I can give you. If I could have offered you more, I would have. The divorce was my fault, as much as the marriage. I never should have asked you to marry me. I was taking advantage of you. I took the lazy way out. In my own bullheaded way, I am trying to give you back your life."

"Noblesse oblige? Gee, Daniel, I never heard you patronize so sweetly."

Slightly embarrassed, Daniel smiled sheepishly. "I guess I should have been honest with you, right from the beginning."

"And now you want to be?" Althea laughed incredulously.

"Yes, actually." He sounded surprised by his admission, but he didn't back down. "I never meant you any harm, I swear it. I asked for the divorce because I didn't want to waste any more of your life. All right, mine, either," he said, seeing her look of suspicion. "But give me some credit, you didn't love me, either."

"I thought I did."

"Perhaps you did. But do you now, upon reflection? Do you still think you did? I don't think so."

Althea's thoughts flew to Harry. "I thought I did," she insisted helplessly.

"Althea, you *never* loved me. You loved what I symbolized, and that was fine, I took you at your word. I admired what *you* signified, too."

"Me?" Althea was astonished. "What could I possibly represent to a man like you? You have everything. Money, status, a powerful family. You're an ambassador, for heaven's sake. I'm just a…a pretty face."

"Your body isn't too bad, either." Daniel grinned.

Finally, a genuine smile, Althea thought. "You're built pretty well yourself," she retorted. "So, great, we have this mutual admiration society. But it made for a lousy marriage."

"This time around, but you underestimate yourself. You are more than the sum of your parts. You're sweet and generous and kind. Fun-loving and friendly. Things I am not. Much more than a face, pretty or otherwise. You didn't get as far as you have because you were dumb."

"I know that."

"I'm not so sure. That's really why I stopped by.

I wanted to tell you that, if you felt in any way at fault for our breakup, I assumed full responsibility, that it was never you. It was a matter of the heart. If the heart is not engaged, it cannot be forced," he said gently as he covered her hand with his. "Please believe me when I tell you, Althea, that I would have loved to fall in love with you. Your pretty face and all," he teased as he flicked her nose. "Trite as it sounds, I would like us to remain friends."

Althea's eyes filled, and Daniel drew her into the fold of his arms. "Yeah, let it out, sweetheart. I came to cry with you. After you left, I realized that we had some unfinished business, that we needed to mourn, I suppose, what could have been. That we had said many things, but we hadn't said goodbye. I loved you, Althea, in my own way, and I still do, my darling. It just isn't the kind of love upon which to build a marriage."

"I know, Daniel, and I love you, too," Althea sniffled as she smoothed down his lapel, neither of them hearing the footsteps that gave way to a voice—an unfriendly voice of deceptive calm.

"Oh, this is too sweet."

Startled, Althea and Daniel both jumped. Harry Bensen stood in the doorway, his mouth set in a crooked grin as he twirled a set of house keys.

"I'll bet you're sorry you gave me these now, darling."

Harry might be smiling, but his eyes were cold

blue stones. Paralyzed, Althea watched as he gently placed the keys on the coffee table and slid them toward her with the tip of a finger.

His diplomatic instincts engaged full force, Daniel rose quickly and held out his hand. "Hi. I'm Daniel Boylan, Althea's ex-husband," he explained with a broad smile. "The ex-husband come to say hello to his ex-wife," he said firmly as he extended his hand.

Harry knew who he was. The ambassador. Looking down at Daniel's outstretched hand, Harry knew the man was doing his best to defuse an awkward situation, and he *wanted* to be persuaded, but the look on Althea's face was too painful to admit any charity. After all, they *had* been wrapped in each other's arms. Ex-husbands wielded a great deal of power.

Dropping his hand, Daniel stepped back.

Harry did, too. One step back, then another, until he turned on his heel, gone before they could stop him.

"Oh, no," Althea said, a shadow of alarm coming over her face. "Did what I think just happened really happen?"

Daniel turned to Althea with a twisted smile. "Did I just ruin your love life?"

"I don't know," she said bleakly.

"Should I go run after that young boy and make him listen to reason?"

"I don't think that's a good idea. He's got a lousy

temper. And that 'young boy' is not as young as you think. In fact, you're exactly the same age. All that hair makes him look like a college kid. No," Althea said, shaking her head, "somehow, I don't think this is the moment to approach him. A cooling-off period is definitely in order. I'll call him tomorrow, talk to him in person."

"Will he listen?" Daniel persisted. "If he won't, you must let me know and I will visit him personally. Ironic, isn't it? Here I was trying to sign a peace treaty with you, and I end up starting a war."

"You do better at the conference table, don't you?" Althea sighed. "Look, Daniel, it's not your fault. Harry ought to trust me more. I gave him my house keys, didn't I? I mean, what on earth is he thinking?"

"If I found you in another man's arms, I might be having the same thoughts, Althea."

"Jeez, you men are so territorial. All that testosterone… Ridiculous."

"It does make for horse races, though."

"Good to know," Althea said wryly. "Next time I go to Saratoga Springs, I'll call you."

"I think you had better call your friend first and ask his permission," Daniel teased, until another thought occurred to him. "How interesting, you're dating a white guy. How did that happen? It seems so out of character."

A bemused smile covered Althea's lips. "Didn't

you say before that it was a matter of the heart? Believe me when I say that dating a white guy was the last thing on my mind. He sort of insisted."

Chapter Sixteen

Althea allowed Daniel to stay overnight in the guest room, but he was gone early the next morning before she woke. He left a note apologizing for his ghostly departure but he was booked on an early flight back to Paris. He would see her next month, when he returned to the States on business. His note was propped against a bouquet of yellow chrysanthemums lying on the kitchen table. Leave it to Daniel to know where to get chrysanthemums at that outrageous hour, Althea thought as she left for work.

Althea took a cab to Harry's house right after work, but he wasn't home. The note she dropped in his mailbox was contrite, as were the phone messages she left on his machine the rest of the week, but in the face of his silence, which grew daily, Althea was forced to ask herself many questions. Her main dilemma was her commitment. There was no doubt in her mind that he would forgive her awkward moment with Daniel. He must know—if he didn't already—that he had misread the situation. But Daniel's visit had seemed to provoke a climax of sorts and Harry's disappearance was definitely connected. She was pretty sure that the question of marriage was on his mind, and *that* decision was implicitly bound with her commitment to her career. Benicia's advice that one could have many careers in one lifetime kept surfacing. The latest muddle had been pushed to the forefront when the Bulgarian model had begun to taunt her, but the blonde was symbolic, because a hundred blondes could pass her way, and Althea would still have to answer the same question—did she really want back in the industry?

Oh, she knew what she'd said, that she was thrilled to be back in the limelight, but when her tired feet dragged her tired body home each evening, her skin irritated by too much makeup, her nerves frayed by too little sleep, she wasn't so sure. Having been forced to think about it by Harry's round of questions, as well as Benicia's, she began to notice the little things.

Like, how she found herself downing way too many aspirins lately, which seemed to bother her stomach more than they cured her headaches.

She found herself resenting the long hours, too, and the stifling working conditions; things that she used to take in her stride.

And she was beginning to have misgivings about going to Morocco. The thought of packing her bags, being trapped in a poorly ventilated plane for twenty hours, the idea of working in a hot climate—a very *hot* climate—was beginning to lose its appeal.

And what about terrorists? They could be anywhere. North Africa suddenly seemed very far away.

When Harry hadn't called her by the end of the week, Althea grew concerned. In a panic, she hurried to Benicia's house after a grueling day of work, even though she longed for her bed. Benicia was thrilled to see her old friend, although she hurried back to the stove where she was boiling potatoes. Althea wasn't all that surprised to see Leonel sitting at the kitchen table, a cup of coffee in one hand and a math book in the other, helping James with his homework. Althea envied their intimate homey setting, and the smell of chicken roasting in the oven made her stomach growl.

"I guess you're staying for dinner," Benicia said, smiling, when she heard her friend's belly rumble.

Althea was hopeful as she threw her coat over the back of a chair. "Do you have enough food?"

"Benicia always has enough food." Leonel laughed as he bussed her cheek. "How you doing, girl?"

"I'm doing fine, thanks. How are you doing, James? Come here and give me a big kiss, sweetie."

James was glad to give the pretty auntie who always smelled so good a great big kiss, although Leonel shooed him right back to his homework. His face in his books, James piped up, surprising Althea with his wide schoolboy smile. "Mr. Murray eats dinner with us *every* night."

"Oh, really?" Althea was openly amused as she plopped beside them at the table. "And does Mr. Murray help you with your homework every night, too?"

"Every night!" James told her proudly. "He's pretty good with vocabulary."

"How about his math?"

"So-so," James said, his voice muffled as he searched for an eraser.

Leonel tried to hide his embarrassment, but it was no use. "Doesn't sound like you're earning your keep." Althea smiled.

"I don't eat here *every* night," Leonel protested.

"Oh, Leonel, why don't you go ahead and tell her?" Benicia said softly, as she mashed the potatoes.

"Tell me what?"

"They're getting married," James snitched from the depths of his math book.

Althea pulled the book down and looked James in the eyes. "No!"

"Yesss!" James grinned, wholly unrepentant. "I'm gonna have a dad," he announced proudly. But his face fell when his mother burst into tears. "What did I do? What did I do? I didn't do nothing!"

Leonel laughed as he gathered Benicia into his arms. "You didn't do *anything*, son. You just took your mother by surprise."

"Me, too." Althea grinned as she hugged James. "This calls for a celebration."

James clapped his hands but Leonel quickly tamped him down. "Sorry, not tonight, young man. You still have a book report to finish, *after* you finish your homework."

"Aw, jeez." But it seemed to Althea that James didn't look at all distressed. She'd bet he probably liked the idea of having a father to give him orders.

"Another time," Althea promised as she squeezed James's hand. "And as for you, miss," she said to Benicia, "why didn't you tell me?" Hugging each other, Benicia wiped away her tears.

"Because it just happened the other night," she said with a pointed look at Leonel. Then, brushing his head with an affectionate hand, she gave Althea the details.

"I'm so excited for you both," Althea said when she heard the story. "Does this mean I get to be a bridesmaid?"

"Maid of honor," Benicia corrected her. "Just as soon as Harry gets back."

"Gets back?" Althea faltered.

"Didn't you know?" Benicia asked with a puzzled frown. "Harry flew down to the Florida Keys, five days ago. He said he wanted to check a story he'd run across about orchids."

"But the Keys are near the Everglades. Isn't that almost like being in a rain forest? Isn't that the very thing his doctors told him not to do?" she spluttered.

"He said he needed to do a little sunbathing, too. Why are you acting like you didn't know? He said he left you a message."

Althea squirmed uncomfortably. Damned phone machines.

Benicia read her one hundred percent. "Let me guess, you didn't listen to your messages."

Althea's laugh was a hollow sound even to her own ears. "Serves me right. But when I get home at night, I'm so tired that half the time I don't even bother to eat. I feel like such a fool."

James was more sympathetic. Jumping from his chair, he scooted over to Althea and wrapped his small arms about her waist. "I love you, Althea."

"Oh, thank you, baby. That means the world to me." Resting her cheek against the top of his head, she sighed.

It caught at Benicia to see her friend so sad, and she sent Leonel a look that said so, but Leonel just shrugged. "Come on, Althea, let's eat. A full stomach always makes things look better."

"Spoken like a man." Althea smiled wanly as Leonel began to set the table while James stowed his schoolbooks on the counter.

But her appetite was gone. Althea picked at her food, making desultory conversation, but her distracted mood wore them all away. Immediately after dinner, Benicia turned to Leonel.

"Leonel," she said quietly as they cleared the table, "maybe you could drive Althea home? I'll help James finish up his book report."

Althea would have preferred to call a cab, she wanted desperately to be alone and think, but Leonel and Benicia wouldn't hear of it. With a quick kiss for James, she and Leonel were soon on the sidewalk, Leonel searching his pockets for his car keys.

"How does it feel to be a couple?" Althea asked, as she slid into the passenger seat.

Leonel shrugged. "I wanted to get engaged the day I met Benicia. She hit me like a rock. But your friend was a hard nut to crack. Finally I broke down her walls. There were times, though, I felt like it was the Norman Conquest."

"She's been a long time building those walls."

"I understood that, but perseverance is my middle name," Leonel said, trying not to sound too proud. "My next job is to talk her into leaving New York. Barring we find a house near Harry, I want out of the city. But she has this job she thinks she can't leave. I told her she was acting like a martyr."

"Oh, she must have loved hearing that."

"It was only a small fight," Leonel sighed. "There are lots of ways to be involved in your community, you know."

"And then there are all those kids you want to have," Althea reminded him.

"There's that, too," Leonel nodded, his face taking on a serious mien.

They drove the rest of the way in silence until Leonel pulled up to Althea's building.

"I feel like I've messed everything up," Althea said sadly.

"You're talking about Harry, I assume?"

Staring out the window, she didn't bother to hide her misery. "I want what's best for him, but if... I said some thoughtless things." Feeling defeated, her hands fell helplessly to her lap. "I kept going on and on about how much I loved my work. I didn't listen when he wanted to talk about his. I even fell asleep one night when he tried," she said sadly, looking at Leonel expectantly.

His lips formed a thin line. "It looks like you have come to the point in life, my dear, where no decision is a bad decision, but a bad decision is going to cost you your happiness."

Althea was thoughtful. "That sounds like double talk. Are you trying to tell me to—"

"Whoa, there, Althea, hold on. I'm not telling you to do anything. You've got to figure that out for yourself. But I have faith in you. You're a real smart woman."

"Actually, not," Althea said with a heavy sigh as she opened the door.

"Ouch." Leonel laughed. "It sounds as if someone is feeling sorry for herself."

Althea's mouth quirked. "Are you always so perceptive?" she asked as she climbed from the car.

"Nah." He smiled. "I can't tell you how many things I've got backward. But it's all part of the game."

A quick phone call to Connie Niles, a few things thrown in an overnight bag, and Althea was on the next plane heading for Miami, two days later. Funny, she thought, as she settled into her seat, how the most crucial moments of her life involved an airline terminal.

During her phone conversation with Connie before she'd left, Connie had not *quite* been angry, but she had owned to being disappointed in Althea's decision to retire. "But you're still a baby," she had moaned.

"That's partly what this is all about. My biological clock is ticking more loudly than usual these days."

"But can't you do both?"

Althea had shaken her head even though Connie hadn't been able to see her. "I don't *want* to do both. I don't *want* to juggle a career and kids and a husband just now. I have a feeling that managing Harry and a kid is going to be a handful."

"You may be right," Connie had agreed after a moment of silence. "But you'll let me know the minute you get bored?"

Wow, great vote of confidence, Althea had thought as she'd hung up. On the other hand, if Harry refused to take her back...

Her conversation with Benicia had been far more supportive. "Of course he'll take you back!" she had protested, hearing the direction Althea's thoughts were heading. "That man is head over heels, to repeat a phrase. Time he was scooped up, and long overdue. And you know what I think? Harry was just waiting for you to get over yourself. I mean, ten years is a long time to *not* get married."

"But look at Leonel," Althea had pointed out.

"Oh, I am, I am." Althea had imagined seeing her friend smile.

"Well then, why do you think *he* waited so long?" she'd asked, the phone tucked between her neck and her ear as she sorted clothes for her trip.

"I know. He's almost forty. I think it was a long-time commitment to his career. The way I figure, he probably got lazy, became a creature of habit. But he claims he was beginning to rethink his priorities before I came into his life."

"He *is* very big on family."

"You noticed?" Benicia chuckled. "It worked out for me because James is the kind of kid you want to have around. If he was the devil's own, I'm not a hundred percent sure that things would have worked out between me and Leonel."

"But Leonel loves you."

"I didn't say he didn't. I know he does, very much, but when a woman has kids, it makes a man think twice about committing, which is how it should be. A woman with kids is a package deal, after all. James—being the nice boy he is, even if I do say so myself—made the wrapping more attractive. Well, he didn't make the wrapping less attractive," Benicia mused.

"I'm going to have children right away," Althea announced. "James Ericson sold himself to more than Leonel."

"That's a sweet thing to say, Althea. But I recommend your getting something glittery on your left hand first. It helps in the long run."

"I'm not going into this thinking about a divorce, Benicia."

"One never does," Benicia agreed quietly. "Make things legal. Believe me, it's better in the long run."

New York's bright winter light could not compete with the burning glare of Miami Beach, and the ensuing two-hour drive down to the Florida Keys in her rental car was unendurable until Althea stopped to purchase sunglasses. Traffic was heavy on US 1, but she made it to Key Largo in under three hours. Switching to the Overseas Highway, she reached Marathon in the late afternoon. Turning onto Sombrero Beach Road, the address Harry had left with Leonel, she drove along the water until she came to a small peninsula jutting into Florida Bay.

Althea was impressed. Pulling off the road, she climbed from her car, enthralled by the sight before her. Bobbing on the dazzling blue-green water of the bay, filling every berth to the point of over-crowding, she was treated to the sight of an elegant collection of sleek and gleaming houseboats. From one small deck to three, they were all of elaborate design and pristine upkeep. Even their names were remarkable. *Jonah's Trawler, Gabby's Gremlin, Carly's Scout About.* Unable to tear her eyes from the shoreline, almost able to taste the saltwater in the air, she was so entranced, she didn't hear Harry's step as he came up behind her.

"Some of these babies even have hot tubs and swim slides," he whispered in her ear.

Althea turned slowly, not surprised by Harry's unromantic greeting. "Some? Not yours?"

Relieved to finally come face-to-face with Harry, she was startled to see how well he looked. Florida seemed to agree with him. His blue eyes were clear, a tan had begun to take, and he had definitely put on weight. Standing in a halo of blazing sun, his mus-cles rippled beneath his T-shirt as he shifted. He had thrived the short week he had spent in Florida. It went a long way to explain his love affair with South America.

"Hell's bells, ma'am," Harry said, "I'm just a poor photographer passing through. Most of these big guys belong to millionaires. I just rented one for the season, but since mine's the sorriest one on the lot, I got a great deal."

Proving his words, Harry strode past Althea to stop abreast the mangiest looking member of millionaire row. No gleaming white paint there. Heck, if she were to guess, the *Jupiter* hadn't seen a paintbrush since it was built, and if it had running hot water, she'd eat her hat. But she wasn't going to criticize the obvious.

"I didn't know Florida could be so beautiful. I thought it was all touristy stuff."

"Yeah, I know what you mean. The drive down US 1 is misleading, and this tiny inlet is so off the main drag, no one comes this way but the locals. I'm impressed that you found me."

"You can thank Leonel for that."

"Yeah, I figured, and I'm going to let him know exactly what I think," Harry said, his displeasure finally making itself known. "What the hell are you doing here, Althea? Is this some sort of dumb joke? It's a good thing Leonel didn't say who the messenger was when he told me he was sending my book by carrier."

"I do not have your book," she said indignantly.

"Bloody hell, Althea, bloody hell."

Althea had to bite her lip from crying, Harry was so angry. "I want to talk. That's why I flew down here, the minute I heard you left. Without even a goodbye," she chided him. "A lousy message on my answering machine. Didn't I deserve better than that?"

But Harry's blue eyes read a flinty *no*. "I have had so many stories from you, Miss Almott, I have been jerked around so much the mind boggles."

"Harry, wait!" Althea cried, catching hold of his shirt. "Won't you even let me explain?"

"Surprise, surprise," Harry said grimly as he peeled away her fingers. "I do not want an explanation. No more stories, not interested. Sayonara, sweetheart." Harry waved as he jumped on board his boat.

"Harry, I quit the business."

Harry's step faltered for a split second, and Althea rushed forward, taking hope. "All my life I've been running in the fast lane. I know that now. There were things I had to do."

"Sorry, Miss Almott, I ain't buying it!" Harry said over his shoulder. But Althea was persistent.

"Harry, other people depended on me—my own mother, for one. My success was her success, my dream was her dream, and we dreamed it way before I ever met you. I couldn't give that up for the sake of a...a man. Men come and go, at least, that's what she taught me. It's what I would have taught my daughter, too, given the circumstances. It's what I will teach my daughters."

Harry was appalled. "That men are unfaithful and undependable?"

"Some men are," said Althea quietly. "Which is why women have to protect themselves. With an education, a career, even a home, if possible. I would teach my children not to wait for anyone—or anything."

"Like you did?" Harry squinted.

"As I said, given the circumstances…"

Harry was unmoved. "Allie, I've heard this all before, and this time it isn't going to fly. Leaving you was never an issue. On the contrary, I wanted to get married, and you know it. But this sure as hell doesn't sound like anything you were saying last week, when you were tired and your guard was down." Harry paused, his smile sardonic. "Let me guess. You've had an epiphany. You finally figured things out."

"Harry Bensen, could you please lose the attitude? I'm trying to tell you that I love you."

"Tell it to the marines."

"Would marrying you be enough?"

Harry was shocked. "Watch out, Althea, I'm not asking you. That was last week."

"You know what, Mr. Bensen? You didn't precisely ask me. But okay, so what, I'm asking *you*."

Harry looked at her long and hard. "What's going on, Allie? You pregnant or something?"

"Not yet, but I'd like to be. Look, Harry, I know I've made mistakes, but I'm trying so hard to undo them, can't you be a little generous? If you leave me now, I don't know what I'll do. Look," she said, thrusting out her left hand, "I'm even wearing your ring on my hand. My left hand, the ring finger."

Looking down at the topaz glittering brighter than the sun, Harry shook his head. "Once upon a time that would have been really nice to know. Sorry, Allie, but I'm leaving in about ten minutes."

"Hey, isn't that a breach of promise?" she shouted as Harry disappeared below.

The hot Florida sun beating down on her head coupled with the bad temper of an intractable man was more than Althea could bear. The bay beckoned, so she dragged herself toward an oasis of green a short distance away, a carpet of grass that skirted the shoreline. A few steps, and she found herself in a small park bordered by tall palm trees, their long elegant branches waving in the offshore breeze. Shucking her shoes, she sank to the cool grass, the fight gone from her as she flopped beneath the soothing shade of a palm tree. Rummaging in her bag, she found her water bottle and sipped slowly as she watched Harry return on deck. When he began to fiddle with some ropes, she didn't smile, and when he glanced her way, she didn't move.

The sun was setting, it was cooling off, and Althea thought it was nice to sit by the water, peaceful, quiet, soothing. Ten minutes later, Harry was surprised to see her still sitting there.

"I'm not going to change my mind, you know," he shouted.

Althea sat motionless, not the slightest hint evident that she had heard him. Her long brown legs stretched before her on the cool grass, she just stared back at him with somber, solemn eyes. From the distance she saw him shrug.

The truth was, she was too tired to respond. And true, too, she had nothing left to say. It was Harry's decision whether to take her back. He was right. She had troubled him enough. When he pulled up anchor, she would leave, but not until he was out of sight. The way he was acting, throwing ropes around and all, he really was going. In a minute or so she would hear the engines start. Or was it a motor? she thought vaguely. What did one call these things? Surprised at the way her mind had drifted, she smiled.

"What's so funny?"

Althea jumped. She must have nodded off, because two hairy, muscle-bound legs had suddenly appeared beside her without warning. Her hands clasped around her water bottle, her words were soft and low as she stared straight ahead. "I won't always get things right, Harry."

"Yeah, well, I've made a few mistakes in my time. Come on, let's go."

Scrambling to her feet, Althea wound her arms around his neck and pressed a soft kiss to his lips. "Were you really going to leave without me?"

"Yeah." Harry smiled as he kissed the tip of her nose. "I'm heading for the Everglades. Then I thought, what with the price of gas, and all," he teased as he drew her closer, "it was cheaper just to take you on now. As my second mate, of course. Although that's not to say there won't be an additional traveler on the way back."

"Excuse me?" Althea asked, her face a picture of confusion.

"You did say you wouldn't mind if you were pregnant, didn't you?" Harry returned, his eyes narrowing.

Althea's face cleared. "Yes, I did, and I meant it."

"Well, good, because that would please me, too." He smiled back. "Only—"

"Only?"

"There's a preacher fellow lives in town. Might be a good idea to stop by before we leave. Matter of fact, I insist. I want to make us legal. You never know when I might have to sue you for child support. You're the one with all the money, don't forget."

"Does that bother you?"

"Hell, no. A rich *and* beautiful wife. What more could a man want?"

"The Pulitzer prize?" Althea asked, her eyebrow a question mark.

"Oh, yeah, that."

"Oh, yeah, *that!*"

Harry scratched at his day-old beard. "That would go a long way toward financial parity, wouldn't it?"

"It would certainly help. Not getting a divorce would help, too." Althea glared.

"Is this our first fight as a married couple?" Harry asked as they strolled toward the houseboat.

Althea's answer was a long-suffering sigh. "We're not married yet, as you pointed out."

"Pure semantics, Allie. Anyway, there's something so sexy about fighting with one's wife." He laughed, jumping back onto the boat deck.

"Where are you going?"

"I have to find my wallet. That preacher will probably want to get paid."

"Oh, Harry, say something romantic, why don't you?" Althea said with a smile.

Harry stopped, his hand on the deck rail, as he looked up at the beautiful woman who had finally come to see things his way. "You mean like 'I'm glad you followed me'?"

"Close but no cigar." She grinned.

"You mean like 'I love you'?"

"That's it," she said happily.

"Oh, Allie, honey," Harry said, his eyes softer than she had ever seen, "I plan to spend the rest of my life telling you how much I love you. Yes, and I think I'll begin right now. Well, as soon as I find my wallet," he said with a wide smile.

* * * * *

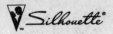

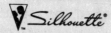

—SPECIAL EDITION™

presents the first book in a compelling
new miniseries by reader favorite

Christine Flynn

GOING HOME

**This quiet Vermont town inspires old lovers
to reunite—and new loves to blossom!**

TRADING SECRETS
SE #1678, available April 2005

Free-spirited, ambitious Jenny Baker thought she'd
left Maple Mountain behind forever. But her city
life didn't go quite as well as she'd planned, and
now Jenny is back home, trying to put her life back
together—and trying to keep the truth about her
return under wraps. Until she's hired by handsome
local doctor Greg Reid, who ignites feelings she'd
thought she'd put to rest long ago. And when
Greg uncovers Jenny's deepest secret, he makes
her an offer she can't refuse....

Where love comes alive™

From

Silhouette

SPECIAL EDITION™

Patricia McLinn

presents her next installment of

Something Old, Something New

LEAST LIKELY WEDDING?
(April 2005, SE #1679)

Kay Aaronson and Rob Dalton couldn't have been more different, but the moment the two opposites met and a pretend kiss became passionate, both knew they were in over their heads. Though they tried to deny it, their attraction was real—until Kay discovered that Rob held the key to revealing a scandal in her family. Would the man she loved destroy her family's reputation?

Available at your favorite retail outlet.

Silhouette®

Where love comes alive™

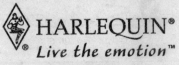